ONCE DORMANT

(A RILEY PAIGE MYSTERY—BOOK 14)

BLAKE PIERCE

BOOKS BY BLAKE PIERCE

PROLOGUE

Gareth Ogden stood on the wide beach looking out over the Gulf of Mexico. The tide was out and the Gulf was calm—the water flat and the waves low. He saw a few seagulls silhouetted against the darkening sky and heard their tired cries over the sound of the waves.

He took a puff of his cigarette and thought with a bitter smile …

The gulls sound like they hate this weather too.

He wasn't sure why he'd even bothered to walk down here from his house. He used to enjoy the sounds and smells of the beach in the evening. Maybe it was just his age, but he found it hard to enjoy much of anything in this muggy heat. Summers were getting hotter than they ever used to. Even after dusk like this, the breeze off the water offered no relieving coolness, and the humidity was suffocating.

He finished his cigarette and ground it into the sand with his foot. Then he turned away from the water to walk back across the waterfront drive toward his house, a weather-beaten structure that looked out over the old road and the desolate beach.

As he trudged across the stretch of sand, Gareth thought of all the repairs he'd had to do on the house after the last hurricane, just a few years back. He'd had to rebuild the big front porch and stairs, and replace a lot of siding and roof shingles, but he'd been lucky that there was no serious structural damage. Amos Crites, who owned the houses on either side of Gareth's, had been faced with almost complete rebuilding.

That goddamn storm, he thought, swatting at a mosquito.

Property values had plummeted since then. He wished he could sell the house and get the hell out of Rushville, but nobody would pay enough for it.

Gareth had lived in this town all his life, and he sure didn't feel like it had done him any favors. As far as he was concerned, Rushville had been going downhill for a long time—at least ever

1

since the interstate had passed it by. He could remember how it had been a thriving little summer tourist town before then, but those days were long gone.

Gareth made his way through an opening in the slatted wooden sand fencing and walked onto the beachfront road. As he felt the soles of his shoes absorb heat from the pavement, he looked up at his house. Its first-floor windows were lit up and friendly ...

Almost like somebody lives there.

Although "living" hardly seemed the word for Gareth's own lonely existence. And thoughts of happier days—when his wife, Kay, was still alive and they were raising their daughter, Cathy—only made him feel more depressed.

As he walked along the sidewalk leading up to his house, Gareth glimpsed something through the screen door—a shadow moving around inside.

Who might that be? he wondered.

He wasn't surprised that some visitor had let himself in. The front door was standing wide open and the screen door was unlatched. Gareth's friends were pretty much free to come and go as they liked.

"It's a free country," he liked to tell them. *"Or so goes the rumor."*

As he climbed the long crooked stairs up to his porch, Gareth figured the visitor might be Amos Crites. Maybe Amos had come over from where he lived on the other side of town to check out his properties along the beach. Gareth knew that nobody had rented either house for August, a notoriously hot and sticky month around here.

Yeah, I'll bet that's who it is, Gareth thought as he crossed the porch.

Amos often stopped by like that to bitch and moan about things in general, and Gareth was glad to chime in with grumbling of his own. He supposed maybe he and Amos were a bad influence on each other that way ...

But hey, what are friends for?

Gareth stood outside the doorway, shaking some sand off his sandals.

"Hey, Amos," he called out. "Grab yourself a beer from the fridge."

He expected Amos to call back ...

"Already got it."

But no reply came. Gareth guessed that maybe Amos was back in the kitchen, just now getting a beer. Or maybe he was just crankier than usual. That was fine with Gareth …

Misery loves company, as they say.

Gareth opened the screen door and walked inside.

"Hey, Amos, what's up?" he called out.

A flash of movement caught his peripheral vision. He turned and glimpsed a shadowy form silhouetted against the living room lamp.

Whoever it was rushed at Gareth too fast for him to ask any questions.

The figure raised an arm, and Gareth glimpsed a flash of steel. Something unspeakably hard crashed against his forehead, and then an explosion burst through his brain like shattering glass.

Then there was nothing.

CHAPTER ONE

Morning sunlight was glistening on the waves as Samantha Kuehling drove the police car along the waterfront drive.

Sitting next to her in the passenger seat, her partner, Dominic Wolfe, said …

"I'll believe it when I see it."

Sam didn't reply.

Neither she nor Dominic yet knew just what "it" really was.

But the truth was, she pretty much believed whatever it was already.

She'd known fourteen-year-old Wyatt Hitt all his life. He could be ornery, just like any boy that age, but he wasn't a liar. And he'd sounded downright hysterical when he'd called the police station a little while ago. He hadn't made much sense, but he'd been pretty clear about one thing …

Something happened to Gareth Ogden.

Something bad.

Beyond that, Sam didn't know a single thing. And Dominic didn't either.

As she parked the car in front of Gareth's house, she saw that Wyatt was sitting at the bottom of the stairs that led up to the porch. Beside him was a cloth bag of undelivered newspapers.

When Sam and Dominic got out of the car and walked over to him, the towheaded kid didn't even look at them. He just kept staring straight ahead. Wyatt's face was even paler than usual, and he was shivering, even though it was already getting to be a hot morning.

He's in shock, Sam realized.

Dominic said to him, "Tell us what happened."

Wyatt sat upright at the sound of Dominic's voice and looked back at him with glazed eyes. Then Wyatt stammered in a hoarse, frightened voice made worse by the changes of adolescence.

"He—he's in there, up in the house. Mr. Ogden, I mean."

Then he stared off toward the Gulf again.

Sam and Dominic looked at each other.

She could tell by Dominic's alarmed expression that this was

4

starting to get real for him.

Sam shuddered as she thought …

I've got a feeling it's about to get awfully real for both of us.

She and Dominic climbed the steps and walked across the porch. When they looked through the screen door, they saw Gareth Ogden.

Dominic staggered backward from the door.

"Jesus Christ!" he yelped.

Ogden was lying on his back on the floor, his eyes and mouth wide open. He had some kind of open, bleeding wound on his forehead.

Then Dominic wheeled back toward the stairs and yelled down at Wyatt …

"What the hell happened? What did you do?"

Feeling a bit surprised not to share Dominic's panic, Sam touched his arm and quietly said, "He didn't do anything, Dom. He's just a kid. He's just a paperboy."

Dominic shook her hand off and stormed back down the stairs. He hauled poor Wyatt to his feet.

"Tell me!" Dominic yelled. "What did you do? Why?"

Sam dashed down the stairs behind Dominic. She grabbed the hysterical cop and forcefully pulled him onto the lawn.

"Leave him alone, Dom," Sam said. "Let me handle this, OK?"

Dominic's face looked as pale as Wyatt's now, and he too was shivering with shock.

He nodded mutely, and Sam walked back over to Wyatt and helped him sit down again.

She crouched in front of him and touched him on the shoulder.

She said, "It's going to be OK, Wyatt. Just take a few slow breaths."

Poor Wyatt couldn't follow her instructions. Instead, he seemed to be hyperventilating and sobbing at the same time.

Wyatt managed to choke out, "I—I came by to deliver his newspaper and I found him in there."

Sam squinted at Wyatt, trying to make sense of this.

"Why did you go all the way up on Mr. Ogden's porch?" she asked. "Couldn't you just throw the paper up there from the yard?"

Wyatt shrugged and said, "He gets—got mad when I do that. It made too much noise, he said, it woke him up. So he told me I had to come all the way up onto the porch—and I had to leave the paper between the screen door and the front door. Otherwise it would blow away, he said. So I always went up there and I was about to open the screen when I saw—"

Wyatt gasped and groaned with shock for a moment, then added …

"So I called you on my cell phone."

Sam patted him on the shoulder.

"It's going to be OK," she said. "You did the right thing, calling the police. Now you wait right here."

Wyatt looked at his bag. "But these papers—I've still got to deliver them."

Poor kid, Sam thought.

He was obviously terribly confused. On top of that, some kind of misplaced guilt seemed to be kicking in as well. Sam guessed that this was a natural reaction.

"You don't have to do anything," she said. "You're not in trouble. Everything's going to be OK. Now just wait here, like I said."

She got up from the step and looked for Dominic, who was still standing dumbly in the yard with his mouth hanging open.

Sam was starting to feel a little angry.

Doesn't he know he's supposed to be a cop?

She said to him, "Dom, come on. We've got to go up there and have a look at things."

Dom just stood there as if he were deaf and had no idea that she'd spoken.

She spoke more sharply. "Dominic, come with me, damn it."

Dominic nodded dumbly, then followed her up the stairs and across the porch into the house.

Gareth Ogden was lying spread-eagle on the floor, wearing sandals and shorts and a T-shirt. The wound in his forehead looked strangely precise and symmetrical. Sam stooped down to get a better look.

Still standing, Dominic stammered, "D-don't touch anything."

Sam almost growled …

"What do you think I am, an idiot?"

What kind of cop didn't know better than to be careful around this kind of a crime scene?

But she looked up at Dominic and saw that he was still pale and trembling.

What if he faints? she thought.

She pointed to a nearby armchair and said, "Sit down, Dom."

Dominic mutely did as he was told.

Sam wondered …

Has he ever seen a dead body before?

Her own experiences were limited to the open-casket funerals of her grandparents. Of course, this was completely different. Even so, Sam felt strangely calm and under control—almost as if she'd been preparing to deal with something like this for a long time.

Dominic obviously wasn't feeling the same way.

She peered closely at the wound in Ogden's forehead. It looked a little bit like that big sinkhole that had collapsed under a country road near Rushville last year—a weird, gaping cavity that didn't belong there.

Weirder still, the skin seemed to be intact—not torn, but stretched into the exact shape of the object that had bashed against it.

It took only a moment for Sam to realize what that object must have been.

She said to Dominic, "Somebody hit him with a hammer."

Apparently feeling less squeamish now, Dominic got up from the chair and knelt beside Sam and looked closely at the corpse.

"How do you know it was a hammer?" he asked.

Half-realizing it sounded like a sick joke, Sam said …

"I know my tools."

In fact, it was true. When she was a little girl, her dad taught her more about tools than most of the boys in town learned in their whole lives. And the indentation of Ogden's wound was the exact shape of the round tip of a perfectly ordinary hammer.

The wound was too big to be made by, say, a ball peen hammer.

Besides, it would have taken a heavier hammer to strike such a deadly single blow.

A claw hammer or a rip hammer, she figured. *One or the other.*

She said to Dominic, "I wonder how the killer got in here."

"Oh, I can tell you that," Dominic said. "Ogden didn't bother to lock his front door much, even when he was gone. He sometimes left it wide open at nights. You know how the folks who live here along the waterfront drive are—dumb and trusting."

Sam found it sad to hear the words "dumb" and "trusting" in the same sentence like that.

Why shouldn't folks be able to leave their houses unlocked in a town like Rushville?

There'd been no violent crime here for years.

Well, they won't be so trusting now, she thought.

Sam said, "The question is, who did this?"

Dominic shrugged and said, "Whoever it was, Ogden sure as hell looks like he was taken by surprise."

Studying the wild look on the corpse's face, Sam silently agreed.

Dominic added, "My guess is it was a total stranger, not somebody from around here. I mean, Ogden was mean, but nobody in town hated him *that* much. And nobody around here's got the makings of a killer. It was probably some drifter who's already come and gone. We'll be damned lucky to catch him."

The thought made Sam's stomach sink.

They couldn't let something like this just happen right here in Rushville.

We just can't.

Besides, she had a strong suspicion that Dominic was wrong.

The killer wasn't just some drifter passing through.

Ogden had been murdered by someone who lived right around here.

For one thing, Sam knew for a fact that this wasn't the first time something had happened right here in Rushville.

But she also knew that now was no time to start speculating.

She said to Dominic, "You call Chief Crane. I'll call the county medical examiner."

Dominic nodded and took out his cell phone.

Before she reached for hers, Sam wiped some sweat off her brow.

It was already getting to be a hot day ...

And it's going to get a whole lot hotter.

CHAPTER TWO

Riley Paige took a long, deep breath of the cool ocean air.

She was sitting on the high porch of a beach house where she, her boyfriend Blaine, and their three teenaged daughters had already spent a week. Down on the wide sandy beach, more summer vacationers were scattered about and others were out in the water. Riley could see April, Jilly, and Crystal playing in the surf. There was a lifeguard on duty, but even so, Riley was glad she had a good view of the girls.

Blaine was lounging in the wicker recliner next to her.

He said, "So are you glad you accepted my invitation to come out here?"

Riley squeezed his hand and said, "Very glad. I could really get used to this."

"I certainly hope so," Blaine said, squeezing her hand back. "When was the last time you took a vacation like this?"

The question took Riley slightly aback.

"I really have no idea," she said. "Years, I guess."

"Well, you've got some catching up to do," Blaine said.

Riley smiled and thought …

Yeah, and another whole week to do it in.

They'd all had a wonderful time so far. A well-to-do friend of Blaine's had offered him the use of his place at Sandbridge Beach for two weeks in August. When Blaine invited them to go along, Riley had realized that she owed it to April and Jilly to spend more time away from work, having fun with them.

Now she thought …

I owed it to myself, too.

Maybe, if she got enough practice in this summer, she'd even get used to pampering herself.

When they'd arrived, Riley had been startled at how elegant this place was, an attractive house raised on pilings and with a wonderful view of the beach from this porch. There was even an outdoor pool in the back.

They'd gotten here just in time to celebrate April's sixteenth birthday. Riley and the girls had spent that day shopping fifteen miles away in Virginia Beach, and they'd visited the aquarium there. Since then they'd barely left this place—and the girls seemed to be anything but bored.

Blaine gently let go of Riley's hand and got up from his chair.

Riley grumbled, "Hey, where do you think you're going?"

"To finish getting dinner ready," Blaine said. Then with an impish grin he added, "Unless you'd rather go out to eat."

Riley laughed at his little joke. Blaine owned a quality restaurant back in Fredericksburg, and he himself was a master chef. He'd been making wonderful seafood dinners ever since they'd gotten here.

"That's out of the question," Riley said. "Now go straight to the kitchen and get to work."

"OK, boss," Blaine said.

He gave her a quick kiss and went on inside. Riley watched the girls romping in the surf for a few moments, then started to feel a little restless and considered going inside to help Blaine with dinner.

But of course, he'd only tell her to come back out here and leave the cooking to him.

So instead, Riley picked up the paperback spy novel she'd been reading. She was too mentally fuzzy right now to make much sense of the elaborate plot, but she was enjoying reading it anyway.

After a little while she felt her whole body twitch, and she realized that she'd dropped the book at her side. She'd fallen asleep for a few minutes—or had it been longer?

Not that it really mattered.

But the afternoon light was waning, and the waves were curling a bit higher. The water looked a little more threatening now that the relentless tide was coming in.

Even with the lifeguard still on duty, Riley felt uneasy. She was about ready to stand up and wave and call out to the girls to tell them it was time to get out of the water, but they seemed to have already come to the same conclusion on their own. They were up on the beach building a sandcastle.

Riley breathed a little easier at their good judgment. At times like now, when the ocean took on a more ominous hue, it occurred to Riley that it wasn't really a place where humans could ever quite belong. Some denizens of the deep were capable of terrible violence—at least as brutal and cruel as the human monsters she hunted and fought as a BAU investigator.

Riley shuddered as she remembered how she'd sometimes had to protect her family against those human monsters. They had been formidable enough. She knew better than to imagine she could ever contend with the monsters of the deep.

Riley's last case had been a full month ago—a string of violent knife murders of rich and powerful men, perpetrated in posh and elegant homes down in Georgia. Since then her professional life had been unusually quiet—and somewhat boring, really.

She'd been updating records, attending meetings, and giving advice to other agents about their cases. But she'd enjoyed giving a couple of lectures to students at the FBI Academy. As a seasoned and even rather celebrated investigator, Riley was a popular lecturer, at least when she was available.

Seeing those young, aspiring faces in the classroom reminded her of her own early idealism, back when she was a trainee in the Academy. Then, she'd been hopeful about the prospect of ridding the world of evildoers. She was a lot less hopeful now, but she was still doing her best.

What else can I do? she asked herself.

It was the only work she knew, and she knew she was very good at her job.

She heard Blaine's voice calling out …

"Riley, dinner is ready. Get the kids."

Riley stood up and waved, shouting "Dinner!" at the top of her lungs.

The girls turned away from their sandcastle, which had become quite elaborate, and they dashed toward the house. They ran underneath the porch where Riley was sitting and to the back of the house, where they could take a quick shower by the swimming pool.

Before she went inside herself, Riley stood by the railing and saw that the girls' sandcastle was already getting nibbled away by the rising tide. Riley couldn't help but feel a tiny bit of sadness about that, but she reminded herself that was normal for castles made of sand.

She'd hardly spent any time at the beach when she was younger. She just hadn't had that kind of a childhood. But from watching the girls playing during the last few days, she knew that part of the fun of building sandcastles was knowing they'd get washed away.

A healthy life lesson, I guess.

She stood watching the sandcastle vanishing into the water for a few moments. When she heard the three girls galloping up the stairs in back, she walked along the porch around the house to meet them.

One was Blaine's sixteen-year-old daughter, Crystal, who was April's best friend. Another was Riley's newly adopted fourteen-year-old daughter, Jilly.

As the three giggling girls started making a dash to their bedroom to change out of their bathing suits for dinner, Riley noticed a small cut on Jilly's thigh.

She gently took Jilly by the arm and said, "How did this happen?"

Jilly glanced at the cut and said, "I dunno. Just got clumsy, I guess. Bumped it into a thorn or something else kind of sharp."

Riley stooped to examine the cut. It wasn't at all bad, and it was already beginning to scab over. Still, it struck Riley as odd somehow. She remembered Jilly having a similar cut on her forearm the day they'd come out here. Jilly had said that April's cat, Marbles, had scratched her. April had denied it.

Jilly drew back from her—a little defensively, Riley thought.

"It's nothing, Mom, OK?"

Riley said, "There's a first aid kit in the bathroom. Put some disinfectant on it before you come to dinner."

"OK, I'll do that," Jilly said.

Riley watched as Jilly ran after April and Crystal to the bedroom.

Nothing to worry about, Riley told herself.

But it was hard not to worry. Jilly had been living with them only since January. When Riley had been working on a case in Arizona, she'd rescued Jilly from desperate circumstances. After some legal and personal struggles, Riley had finally been able to adopt Jilly just a month ago, and Jilly seemed happy with her new family.

And besides …

It's just a little cut—nothing to worry about.

Riley went to the kitchen to help Blaine set the table and put dinner on. The girls soon joined them, and they all sat down to dinner—delicious fried flounder filets served with tartar sauce. Everybody was happy and laughing. By the time Blaine served cheesecake for dessert, a warm, pleasant feeling was coming over Riley.

We're like a family, she thought.

Or maybe that wasn't quite right. Maybe, just maybe …

We really are *a family.*

It had been a long time since Riley had felt like that.

As she finished her dessert, she thought again …

I could really get used to this.

*

After supper, the girls went back to their bedroom to play games before going to sleep. Riley joined Blaine on the porch, where they sipped glasses of wine as they watched night setting in. The two of them were quiet for a long time.

Riley basked in that quietness, and she sensed that Blaine did too.

She couldn't remember having shared many easy, comfortable, silent moments like this with her ex-husband, Ryan. They'd pretty much always either been talking or deliberately not talking. And when they hadn't been talking, they'd simply inhabited their own separate worlds.

But Blaine felt very much a part of Riley's world right now …

And a beautiful world it is.

The moon was bright, and as the night grew darker, stars were appearing in huge clusters—almost unbelievably bright out here away from the lights of the city. The dark waves of the Gulf reflected the light of the moon and the stars. Far away, the horizon grew blurry and finally disappeared so that the sea and the sky seemed to blend seamlessly together.

Riley shut her eyes and listened for a moment to the sound of the surf.

There were no other noises at all—no voices, no TV, no city traffic.

Riley sighed a long, deep, happy sigh.

As if answering her sigh, Blaine said …

"Riley, I've been wondering …"

He paused. Riley opened her eyes and looked over at him, feeling just a twinge of apprehension.

Then Blaine continued …

"Do you feel like we've known each other for a long time, or just a short time?"

Riley smiled. It was an interesting question. They'd known

each other for about a year now, and they'd declared themselves exclusive about three months ago. During all that time they'd become very comfortable together.

They and their families had also been through moments of harrowing danger, and Blaine had shown amazing resourcefulness and courage.

Through it all, Riley had come to care about him, trust him, and admire him.

"It's hard to say," she said. "Both, I guess. It seems like a long time because of how close we've gotten. It seems like a short time because … well, because I'm sometimes so amazed at how fast we've gotten so close."

Another silence fell—a silence that told Riley that Blaine felt exactly the same way.

Finally Blaine said …

"What do you think … should happen next?"

Riley looked into his eyes. His gaze was earnest and inquisitive.

Riley smiled and said the first thing that popped into her head. "Why, Blaine Hildreth—are you proposing to me?"

Blaine smiled and said, "Come on inside. I've got something to show you."

CHAPTER THREE

Riley felt a bit breathless now. A whole world of future possibilities seemed to be opening up in front of her, and she didn't have any idea how to think about them.

She didn't know what to say, so she just picked up her glass of wine and followed Blaine off the porch into the dining room.

Blaine went to a cabinet and took out a large roll of paper. When they'd arrived, Riley had noticed him unpacking the roll from the car along with beach stuff, but she hadn't bothered to ask him what it was.

He unrolled the sheet on the dining room table, putting cups on the corners to hold it down. It looked like some kind of elaborate ground plan.

"What is this?" Riley asked.

"Don't you recognize it?" Blaine said. "It's my house."

Riley looked at the drawings more carefully, feeling slightly puzzled.

She said, "Um … it looks awfully big to be your house."

Blaine chuckled and said, "That's because a whole wing of it hasn't been built yet."

Riley felt positively dizzy as Blaine began to explain the drawings. He showed how the new wing would include bedrooms for April and Jilly. And of course there would be an entire apartment for Gabriela, Riley's live-in housekeeper, who could work for them all once everything was built. The new design even included a small office for Riley. She hadn't had a home office since Jilly had moved in and they'd needed it for a bedroom.

Riley was both overwhelmed and amused.

When he finished explaining things, she said …

"So—is this your way of asking me to marry you?"

Blaine stammered, "I—I guess it is. I realize it's not very romantic. No ring, no kneeling."

Riley laughed and said, "Blaine, if you kneel, I swear to God I'll slap you silly."

Blaine stared at her with surprise.

But Riley almost meant it. She was having a flashback to Ryan proposing to her so many years ago when they'd been young and poor—Ryan a struggling lawyer and Riley an FBI intern. Ryan had gone through the whole ritual, kneeling and offering her a ring that he really couldn't afford.

It had seemed plenty romantic back then.

But things had turned out so badly for them, the memory seemed sour to Riley now.

Blaine's much less traditional proposal seemed perfect by comparison.

Blaine put his arm around Riley's shoulders and kissed her on the neck.

"You know, marriage would have practical advantages," he said. "We wouldn't have to sleep in separate bedrooms when the kids were around."

Riley felt a tingle of desire at his kiss and his suggestion.

Yes, that would be an advantage, she thought.

Intimate moments had been scarce. The two of them had relegated themselves to separate bedrooms even during this lovely vacation.

Riley sighed deeply and said, "It's a lot to think about, Blaine. A lot for both of us to think about."

Blaine nodded. "I know. That's why I don't expect you to jump up and down with joy yelling 'yes, yes, yes' at the top of your lungs. I just want you to know … it's been on my mind, and I hope it's been on your mind too."

Riley smiled and admitted, "Yes, it has been on my mind."

They looked into each other's eyes for a few moments. Again, Riley found herself enjoying the quietness between them. But of course, she knew they couldn't leave all those questions milling through both their minds unanswered.

Finally Riley said, "Let's go back outside."

They refilled their glasses and went out onto the porch and sat down again. The night was getting lovelier by the minute.

Blaine reached over and took Riley's hand. "I know it's a big decision. We've got a lot to think over. For one thing, we've both been married before. And … well, we're not getting any younger."

Riley silently thought …

All the more reason to make a commitment.

Blaine continued, "Maybe we should start by listing all the reasons why this might not be a good idea."

Riley laughed and said, "Oh, Blaine—do we have to?"

But she knew perfectly well he was right.

And I might as well be the one to start, she decided.

She took a long, slow breath and said, "To begin with, we've got more than each other to think about. We're already both parents, with three teenagers between us. If we get married we'll also be stepparents—me to your girl, you to my two girls. That's quite a commitment right there."

"I know," Blaine said. "But I love the idea of being a father to April and Jilly."

Riley's throat tightened with emotion at the sincerity in his voice.

"I feel the same way about Crystal," she said. Then with a chuckle she added, "My girls have already got a cat and a dog. I hope that's OK."

Blaine said, "That's fine. I won't even ask for a pet deposit."

Their laughter rang musically through the night air.

Then Riley said, "OK, it's your turn."

Blaine sighed deeply and said, "Well, we've both got exes."

Echoing his sigh, Riley said, "That we do."

She shuddered as she remembered her only encounter with Blaine's ex-wife, Phoebe. The woman had been physically attacking poor Crystal in a drunken rage until Riley pulled her off.

Blaine had told Riley that his marriage to Phoebe had been a mistake of his youth, before he'd had any idea that she was bipolar and a danger to herself and others.

Seeming to guess Riley's thoughts, Blaine said …

"I never hear from Phoebe anymore. She's living with her sister, Drew. I do communicate with Drew from time to time. She says Phoebe is in recovery and doing better, but she doesn't give any thought to Crystal and me anymore. I'm sure she's out of our lives for good."

Riley swallowed hard and said …

"I wish I could say the same for Ryan."

Blaine squeezed Riley's hand and said, "Well, he is April's father. He's going to want to keep being part of your lives. Jilly's too. I can understand that."

"You're being too fair to him," Riley said.

"Really? Why?"

Riley thought …

How can I begin to explain?

Ryan's one attempt to reconcile and move back in with her had ended disastrously—especially for Jilly and April, who learned the hard way they couldn't rely on him to be any kind of a father.

Meanwhile, Riley had no idea how many girlfriends had come and gone in Ryan's life.

She took a sip of her wine and said, "I don't think we'll see much of Ryan. And I think that's just as well."

Riley and Blaine fell silent for a few moments. As they stared out into the night, Riley's worries about Phoebe and Ryan slipped out of her mind, and again she basked in the wonderful warmth and comfort of Blaine's simple companionship.

The quiet was broken by the sounds of footsteps and chattering and giggling as the girls came running out of their room. Then it sounded like they were doing something in the kitchen—getting a late-night snack, Riley guessed.

Meanwhile, Riley and Blaine started talking quietly about different issues—how their very different careers might or might not mesh, how Riley would have to sell the townhouse she'd bought just a year ago, how they would manage their finances, and similar things.

As they talked, Riley found herself thinking …

We started off trying to list reasons why getting married isn't a good idea.

Instead, it seemed like a better and better idea with each passing second.

And the really beautiful thing was—neither of them had to say so aloud.

I might as well have said yes, she thought.

She certainly felt as though they were seriously engaged to be married.

And she really liked that feeling.

Their conversation was broken when April came rushing out onto the porch with Riley's cell phone in hand.

The phone was buzzing.

Handing the phone to Riley, April said …

"Hey, Mom—you left your phone in the kitchen. You've got a call."

Riley stifled a sigh. She couldn't imagine that the call was from anyone she'd want to hear from right now. Sure enough, she saw that the caller was her boss, Special Agent Brent Meredith.

Her spirits faded as she realized …

He wants me back at work.

CHAPTER FOUR

When Riley answered the call, she heard Meredith's familiar gruff voice.

"How's your vacation going, Agent Paige?"

Riley managed to keep from saying ...

"It was going fine until just now."

Instead she replied, "It's lovely. Thanks."

She got up from the chair and wandered along the porch a little ways.

Meredith let out a hesitant growl, then said ...

"Listen, we've been getting some peculiar phone calls from a female police officer in Mississippi—a little beachside town called Rushville. She's working on a murder case. A local man got his head bashed in with a hammer and ..."

Meredith paused again, then said ...

"She's got some idea that they're dealing with a serial killer."

"Why?" Riley asked.

"Because something similar happened in Rushville—some ten years ago."

Riley's squinted with surprise.

She said, "That's kind of a long time between murders."

"Yeah, I know," Meredith said. "I talked to her chief, and he said there was nothing to it. He said she's just some bored small-town cop looking for excitement. The thing is, though, she keeps calling and she doesn't really sound like a crazy person so maybe ..."

Again Meredith fell silent. Riley looked inside the house and saw that Blaine was helping the girls get something to eat in the kitchen. They all looked so happy. Riley's heart sank at the thought of having to cut things short.

Then Meredith said, "Look, I guess I was just thinking, if you're tired of vacationing and feeling homesick for work, maybe you could go down to Mississippi and—"

Riley was startled to hear her own voice interrupt him sharply.

"No," she said.

Another silence fell, and Riley's heart jumped up into her throat.

Oh, my God, she thought.

I just said no to Brent Meredith.

She couldn't remember ever having done that before—and for very good reason. Meredith was known to have a sharp dislike for that word, especially when there was a job to do.

Riley braced herself for a fierce dressing-down. Instead, she heard a gravelly sigh.

Meredith said, "Yeah, I should have figured. It's probably nothing anyway. I'm sorry I bothered you. Keep on enjoying your vacation."

Meredith ended the call, and Riley stood on the porch looking at the phone.

Meredith's words rattled through her head ...

"I'm sorry I bothered you."

That didn't sound like the chief at all.

Apologies of any sort just weren't his style.

So what was he really thinking?

Riley had a feeling that Meredith didn't believe what he'd just said ...

"It's probably nothing anyway."

Riley suspected that something about the female cop's story had piqued Meredith's interest, and he more than half believed there really was a serial killer down in Mississippi. But because he didn't have any tangible evidence to go on, he didn't feel as though he could just haul off and order Riley to take the case.

As Riley kept staring at the phone she found herself thinking ...

Should I maybe call him back?

Should I go to Mississippi and check this out, at least?

Her thoughts were interrupted by April's voice.

"So what's going on? Is vacation over?"

Riley looked and saw that her daughter was standing nearby on the porch, looking at her with a sour expression.

"Why do you think that?" Riley asked.

April sighed and said, "Come on, Mom. I saw who the call was from. You've got to run off on another case, don't you?"

Riley looked into the kitchen and saw that Blaine and the other two girls were still putting snacks together. But Jilly was eyeing Riley uneasily.

Riley suddenly wondered ...

What the hell was I just thinking?

She smiled at April and said ...

"No, I don't have to go anywhere. As a matter of fact ..."

Then smiling more broadly she added ...

"I said no."

April's eyes widened. Then she dashed back into the kitchen shouting ...

"Hey, guys! Mom said no to a case!"

The other two girls started yelling "Yay!" and "Way to go!" while Blaine gazed at Riley happily.

Then some lighthearted bickering started as Jilly said to her sister ...

"I told you. I told you she'd say no."

April retorted, "No, you didn't. You were even more worried than I was."

"Was not," Jilly said. "You owe me ten dollars."

"We never made a bet about it!"

"Did too!"

The two girls punched each other playfully, giggling and laughing as they argued.

Riley laughed as well and said, "OK, kids. Break it up. No arguing. Don't spoil a perfect vacation. Let's all have something to eat."

She joined the chattering, laughing group for an evening snack.

As they ate, she and Blaine kept looking at each other lovingly.

They really were a couple with three teenaged children to raise.

Riley wondered ...

When was the last time I had a night this wonderful?

*

Riley was barefoot, walking on a stretch of beach as the morning light gleamed on the waves. The gulls were calling and the breeze was cool and gentle.

It's going to be a beautiful day, *she thought.*

But even so, something seemed deeply wrong.

It took her a moment to realize ...

I'm alone.

She looked up and down the beach and saw no one as far as she could see.

Where are they? *she wondered.*

Where were April and Jilly and Crystal?

21

And where was Blaine?

A strange dread started to rise up in her, and also a terrifying thought ...

Maybe I dreamed the whole thing.

Yes, maybe last night had never happened.

None of it.

Those loving moments with Blaine as they planned their future together.

The laughter of her two daughters—and also Crystal, who was about to become her third daughter.

Her warm, rich feeling of belonging—a feeling she'd spent her whole life seeking and craving.

All just a dream.

And now she was alone—as alone as she'd ever been in her life.

Just then she heard laughing and chattering behind her.

She spun around and saw them ...

Blaine, Crystal, April, and Jilly were all running around throwing a beach ball to one another.

Riley breathed a deep sigh of relief.

Of course it was real, *she thought.*

Of course I didn't just imagine it.

Riley laughed with joy and broke into a run to join them.

But then something hard and invisible stopped her dead in her tracks.

It was some kind of a barrier that separated her from the people she loved most.

Riley walked along the barrier, running her hands along it, thinking ...

Maybe there's a way around it.

Then she heard a familiar rasp of laughter.

"Give it up, girl," a voice said. "That life's not for you."

Riley turned around and saw someone standing just a few feet away from her.

It was a man in the full-dress uniform of a Marine colonel. He was tall and gangly, his face worn and wrinkled from years of anger and alcohol.

He was the last human being in the world Riley wanted to see.

"Daddy," she murmured with despair.

He chuckled grimly and said, "Hey, you don't have to sound so goddamn sad about it. I thought you'd be glad to be reunited with your own flesh and blood."

"You're dead," Riley said.

Daddy shrugged and said, "Well, as you already know, that doesn't stop me from checking in from time to time."

Riley dimly realized that this was the truth.

This wasn't the first time she'd seen her father since his death last year.

And this wasn't the first time she'd been puzzled by his presence. Just how she could be talking to a dead man made no real sense to her.

But she did know one thing for sure.

She wanted nothing to do with him.

She wanted to be among people who didn't make her hate herself.

She turned and started to walk toward Blaine and the girls, who were still playing with the beach ball.

Again she was stopped by that invisible barrier.

Her father laughed. "How many times have I got to tell you? You've got no business with them."

Riley's whole body shook—whether with rage or heartbreak, she wasn't sure.

She turned toward her father and yelled ...

"Leave me alone!"

"Are you sure?" he said. "I'm all you've got. I'm all you are."

Riley snarled, "I'm nothing like you. I know what it means to love and be loved."

Her father shook his head and shuffled his feet in the sand.

"It's not that I don't sympathize," he said. "It's a damn crazy useless life you've got—seeking justice for people who're already dead, exactly the people who don't need justice anymore. Just like it was for me in 'Nam, a stupid war there was no way to win. But you've got no choice, and it's time to make peace with it. You're a hunter, like me. I raised you that way. We don't know anything else—neither one of us."

Riley locked eyes with him, testing her will against his.

Sometimes she could best him, making him blink.

But now wasn't one of those times.

She blinked and looked away.

Her father sneered at her and said, "Hell, if you want to be alone, that's fine with me. I'm not exactly enjoying your company either."

He turned and walked away down the beach.

Riley turned around, and this time she saw them all walking away—April and Jilly hand in hand, Blaine and Crystal heading their own separate way.

As they started to disappear in the morning missed, Riley pounded on the barrier and tried to shout ...

"Come back! Please come back! I love you all!"

Her lips moved but made no sound at all.

*

Riley eyes snapped open and she found herself lying in bed.

A dream, she thought. *I should have known it was a dream.*

Her father sometimes came to her in dreams.

How else could he visit her, being dead?

It took her another moment to realize that she was crying.

The overwhelming loneliness, the isolation from the people she loved most, the words of warning from her father ...

"You're a hunter, like me."

Small wonder she'd woken up in such distress.

She reached for a tissue and managed to calm her sobbing. But even then, that lonely feeling wouldn't go away. She reminded herself that the kids were sleeping in another room, and Blaine was in another.

But it seemed hard to believe somehow.

Alone in the dark, she felt as though any other people were far away, on the other side of the world.

She thought about getting up and tiptoeing down the hall and joining Blaine in his room, but ...

The kids.

They were staying in separate bedrooms because of the kids.

She tugged the pillow around her head and tried to go to sleep again, but she couldn't stop thinking ...

A hammer.

Someone in Mississippi got killed with a hammer.

She told herself it wasn't her case, and she'd said no to Brent Meredith.

But even as she finally drifted back to sleep, those thoughts wouldn't go away ...

There's a killer out there.

There's a case to be solved.

24

CHAPTER FIVE

When she walked into the Rushville police station first thing in the morning, Samantha had a feeling she was going to be in trouble. Yesterday she'd made a few phone calls that perhaps she shouldn't have made.

Maybe I should learn to mind my own business, she thought.

But somehow, minding her own business didn't come easily to her.

She was always trying to fix things—sometimes things that couldn't be fixed, or things that other people didn't want to have fixed.

As usual when she showed up for work, Sam saw no other cops around, just the chief's secretary, Mary Ruckle.

Her fellow officers teased her a lot for that …

"Good old reliable Sam," they'd say. *"Always the first to get here, the last to get out."*

Somehow, they never seemed to mean that in a nice way. But she always reminded herself that it was natural for "good old reliable Sam" to get picked on. She was the youngest and newest cop on the Rushville force. It didn't help any that she was also the only female on the force.

For a moment Mary Ruckle didn't seem to notice Sam's arrival. She was busily doing her nails—her usual occupation during most of a workday. Sam couldn't understand the appeal of doing one's nails. She always kept hers plain and clipped short, which was maybe one of the many reasons people thought of her as, well …

Unladylike.

Not that Mary Ruckle was what Sam would consider attractive. Her face was all tight and mean, as if it were all pinched together by a clothespin on the bridge of her nose. Still, Mary was married with three children, and few people in Rushville foresaw that kind of life for Sam.

Whether Sam actually wanted that kind of life, she didn't really know. She tried not to think too much about the future. Maybe that was why she focused so hard on every bit of whatever came in front of her on any given day. She couldn't actually imagine a future for herself, at least not among the choices that seemed to be available.

Mary puffed on her nails and looked up at Sam and said …

"Chief Crane wants to talk to you."

Sam nodded with a sigh.

Just like I expected, she thought.

She walked on into the chief's office and found Chief Carter Crane playing Tetris on his computer.

"Just a minute," he grumbled upon hearing Sam walk into the room.

Probably distracted by Sam's arrival, he quickly lost the game he was playing.

"Damn," he said, staring at the screen.

Sam braced herself. He was probably already pissed off with her. Blowing a game of Tetris wasn't going to improve his mood.

The Chief turned around in his swivel chair and said …

"Kuehling, sit."

Sam obediently sat down in front of his desk.

Chief Crane steepled his fingertips together and stared at her for a moment, trying as usual to look like the big shot he imagined himself to be. And as usual, Sam wasn't impressed.

Crane was about thirty, and he was blandly pleasant-looking in a way that Sam thought would better suit an insurance man. Instead, he had risen to the post of police chief due to the power vacuum that Chief Jason Swihart had left when he went suddenly went away two years ago.

Swihart had been a good chief and everybody had liked him, including Sam. Swihart been offered a great job with a security company way over in Silicon Valley, and he'd understandably moved on to greener pastures.

So now Sam and the other cops were answerable to Chief Carter Crane. As far as Sam was concerned, he was a mediocrity in a department full of mediocrities. Sam would never admit it aloud, but she felt sure she had better brains than Crane and all the other local cops put together.

It'd be nice to have a chance to prove it, she thought.

Finally Crane said, "I got an interesting phone call last night— from a certain Special Agent Brent Meredith in Quantico. You'd never believe what he told me. Oh, but then again, maybe you would."

Sam groaned with annoyance and said, "Come on, Chief. Let's

get right to the point. I called the FBI late last afternoon. I talked to several people before I finally got connected with Meredith. I thought somebody ought to call the FBI. They should be down here helping us out."

Crane smirked and said, "Don't tell me. It's because you still think Gareth Ogden's murder the night before last was the work of a serial killer who lives right here in Rushville."

Sam rolled her eyes.

"Do I need to explain it all over again?" she said. "The whole Bonnett family got killed here one night ten years ago. Somebody bashed in their heads with a hammer. The case was never solved."

Crane nodded and said, "And you think the same killer has come out of the woodwork ten years later."

Sam shrugged and said, "There's pretty obviously some connection. The MO is identical."

Crane suddenly raised his voice a little.

"There's no connection. We went through all this yesterday. The MO is just a coincidence. The best we can tell, Gareth Ogden was killed by some drifter passing through town. We're following every lead we can. But unless he does the same thing somewhere else, we're liable to never catch him."

Sam felt a surge of impatience.

She said, "If he was just a drifter, why wasn't there any sign of a robbery?"

Crane slapped his desk with the palm of his hand.

"Damn it, you don't give up on any of your notions, do you? We don't know that there *wasn't* a robbery. Ogden was dumb enough to leave his front door open. Maybe he was also dumb enough to leave a wad of money lying on his coffee table. The killer saw it and decided to help himself to it, bashing in Ogden's head in the process."

Cradling his fingertips together again, Crane added …

"Now doesn't that sound more plausible than some psychopath who's spent ten long years … doing what, exactly? Hibernating, maybe?"

Sam took a long, deep breath.

Don't get started with him again, she told herself.

There was no point in explaining all over again just why Crane's theory bugged her. For one thing, what about the hammer? She herself had noticed that Ogden's hammers were all still neatly stowed in his tool chest. So did the killer lug around a hammer with him as he drifted from town to town?

It was possible, sure.

It also struck her as a little bit ridiculous.

Crane growled sullenly and added, "I told that Meredith guy that you were bored and overly imaginative and to forget all about it. But frankly, the whole conversation was embarrassing. I don't like it when people go over my head. You had no business making those phone calls. Asking for help from the FBI is my job, not yours."

Sam was grinding her teeth, struggling to keep her thoughts to herself.

She managed to say in a quiet voice …

"Yes, Chief."

Crane breathed what sounded like a sigh of relief.

"I'm going to let this slide and not take any disciplinary action this time around," he said. "The truth is, I'd be much happier if none of the guys found out any of this happened. Have you told anybody else here about your shenanigans?"

"No, Chief."

"Then keep it that way," Crane said.

Crane turned and started a new game of Tetris as Sam left his office. She went to her desk and sat down and brooded silently.

If I can't talk to somebody about this, I'm liable to explode, she thought.

But she'd just promised not to bring it up with the other cops.

So who did that leave?

She could think of exactly one person … the one who was the reason she was here, trying to do this job …

My dad.

He'd been an active duty cop here when the Bonnett family had been murdered.

The fact that the case wasn't solved had haunted him for years.

Maybe Dad could tell me something, she thought.

Maybe he'd have some ideas.

But Sam's heart sank as she realized that wouldn't be such a good idea. Her father was in a local nursing home and was suffering from bouts of dementia. He had his good days and his bad days, but bringing up a case from his past would almost certainly upset and confuse him. Sam didn't want to do that.

Right now she had nothing much to do until her partner, Dominic, showed up for their morning beat. She hoped he'd get

28

here soon, so they could make a round of the area before the heat got too oppressive. Today was expected to break some records.

Meanwhile, there was no point in worrying about things she couldn't do anything about—not even the possibility that a serial killer might be right here in Rushville, getting ready to strike again.

Try not to think about it, she told herself.

Then she scoffed and murmured aloud …

"Like *that's* going to happen."

CHAPTER SIX

Riley's cell phone buzzed while Blaine was driving them all back to Fredericksburg. She was surprised and unsettled to see who the call was from.

Is this some kind of emergency? she wondered.

Gabriela never called her just to chat, and she had made a point of not calling at all during their two weeks at the beach. She'd only sent an occasional text to let Riley know that everything was all right at home.

Riley's concern grew when she took the call and heard a note of alarm in Gabriela's voice …

"Señora Riley—when will you be home?"

"In about half an hour," Riley said. "Why?"

She heard Gabriela inhale sharply, then say …

"He's here."

"Who's here?" Riley asked.

When Gabriela didn't answer immediately, Riley understood …

"Oh my God," she said. "Ryan's there?"

"Sí," Gabriela said.

"What does he want?" Riley asked.

"He does not say. But he says it is something important. He is waiting for you."

Riley almost asked Gabriela to put Ryan on the phone. But then it occurred to her—whatever Ryan wanted was probably nothing she'd want to discuss on the phone right now. Not with everybody else right there in the car.

Instead Riley said, "Tell him I'll be home soon."

"I will," Gabriela said.

They ended the call and Riley sat staring out the SUV window.

After a moment Blaine said, "Um … did I hear you say something about …?"

Riley nodded.

Sitting behind them listening to music, the girls hadn't been listening until just now.

"What?" April asked. "What's going on?"

Riley sighed and said, "It's your father. He's at home waiting for us."

Both April and Jilly gasped aloud.

Then Jilly said, "Couldn't you tell Gabriela to just make him go away?"

Riley was tempted to say she'd really like to, but it wouldn't be fair to unload that task on Gabriela.

Instead she said …

"You know I can't do that."

April and Jilly both moaned with dismay.

Riley could well understand how her two daughters felt. Ryan's last unannounced visit to their house had been unpleasant for everybody—Ryan included. His attempt to charm his way back into the girls' lives had backfired. April had been cool toward him, and Jilly had been downright rude.

Riley hadn't been able to blame either one of them.

One too many times, Ryan had built up their hopes that he could still act like a father. He'd dashed those hopes yet again, and the girls had wanted nothing to do with him.

What does he want now? Riley wondered, sighing again.

Whatever it was, she hoped it wasn't going to sour everybody's good feelings about the vacation they'd just had. It had been a lovely two weeks, despite Riley's dream about her father. Since then she had done her best to put Agent Meredith's call out of her mind.

But now the news about Ryan seemed to trigger her dark thoughts again.

A hammer, she thought.

Someone was killed with a hammer.

She reminded herself sternly that she'd done the right thing by saying no to Chief Meredith. Besides, he hadn't called her again about it, which surely meant that he wasn't very concerned about it after all.

It was probably nothing, she thought.

Just a case for the locals to take care of.

*

Everybody's anxiety mounted as Blaine pulled his SUV up in front of Riley's townhouse. An expensive Audi was parked out in front. It was Ryan's car, of course—but Riley couldn't remember whether it was the same car he'd had the last time he'd been here. He liked to keep up on the latest models, no matter how expensive.

Once they were parked, Blaine stammered awkwardly. He wanted to help Riley and her two daughters carry their bags back into the house, but …

"Is it going to be awkward?" Blaine asked Riley.

Riley stifled a groan.

Of course, she thought.

Blaine and Ryan had rarely met, but those encounters had hardly been friendly—at least on Ryan's part. Blaine had done his best to be pleasant, but Ryan had been sullen and hostile.

Riley and April and Jilly could easily carry their bags inside in a single trip. They didn't really need Blaine's help, and Riley didn't want Blaine to feel uncomfortable, and yet …

Why the hell should Blaine feel uncomfortable in my own house?

Telling Blaine and Crystal to go away was no solution to this problem.

Riley said to Blaine, "Come on in."

The group carried all the bags into the house. Gabriela met them at the door, along with Jilly's small, big-eared dog, Darby. The dog bounced around them with delight, but Gabriela didn't look nearly so happy.

As they put the bags down in the entry area, Riley saw Ryan sitting in the living room. Riley was alarmed to see that he was flanked by two suitcases …

Is he planning to stay?

April's black and white kitten, Marbles, lay comfortably in his lap.

Ryan looked up from petting Marbles.

He smiled weakly and said in a rather pathetic voice …

"A kitten and a dog! Wow, all this is new!"

With a gasp of annoyance, April snatched Marbles out of Ryan's lap.

Ryan looked hurt, of course. But again, Riley understood well how April felt.

As April and Jilly both headed toward the stairs, Riley said …

"Hold on, girls. Don't you have something to say to Blaine and Crystal?"

Looking a little ashamed at their lapse of manners, April and Jilly thanked Blaine and Crystal for the great time they had.

Crystal gave each of the other girls a hug. "Call you tomorrow," she said to April.

"Now take your stuff up with you," Riley told them.

April and Jilly obediently grabbed their bags. Jilly picked up most of their other things, since April was still holding Marbles in one hand. Then they both headed up the stairs, and Darby scampered after them. Seconds later came two banging sounds as they shut their bedroom doors behind them.

Gabriela looked at Ryan with dismay and headed away to her own apartment.

Ryan looked at Blaine and said timidly, "Hi, Blaine. Hope you all had a good vacation."

Riley's mouth dropped open with surprise.

He's trying to be polite, she thought.

Now she knew that something must be terribly wrong.

Blaine gave Ryan a small wave and said, "It was great, Ryan. How have you been?"

Ryan shrugged and said nothing.

Riley was determined not to let Ryan limit her behavior.

She kissed Blaine gently on the lips and said, "Thanks for the wonderful time."

Blaine blushed, obviously embarrassed by the situation.

"Thank you—and your girls," he said.

Crystal shook Riley's hand and thanked her.

Blaine mouthed silently to Riley, "Call me later."

Riley nodded yes, and Blaine and his daughter headed on out to his SUV.

Riley took a deep breath and turned to face the only other person left in the living room. Her ex-husband stared silently at her with pleading eyes.

What does he want? she wondered yet again.

Usually when Ryan came around, she'd be aware right away that he was still a handsome man—somewhat taller, older, and more athletic than Blaine, and always perfectly groomed and dressed. But this time was somehow different. He looked rumpled and sad and broken. She'd never seen him look this way.

Riley was about to ask him what was wrong when he said …

"Could we maybe have a drink?"

Riley looked at his face for a moment. It was drawn and sallow. She wondered …

Has he been drinking lately?

Did he have a few drinks before coming here?

She briefly considered denying his request, but then headed out to the kitchen and poured bourbon on ice for both of them. She brought the drinks out into the living room and sat down in a chair facing him, waiting for him to say something.

Finally, with his shoulders hunched, he said in a hushed voice …

"Riley—I'm ruined."

Riley's mouth dropped open.

What does he mean? she wondered.

CHAPTER SEVEN

As Riley sat there staring at him, Ryan said the words again ...

"I'm ruined. My whole life is ruined."

Riley was stunned. She couldn't remember the last time he'd spoken in such a despondent tone. Arrogance and self-confidence were more his style.

"What do you mean?" she asked.

He heaved a long, miserable sigh and said, "Paul and Barrett— they're forcing me out of the firm."

Riley could hardly believe her ears.

Paul Vernasco and Barrett Gaynor had been Ryan's law partners ever since the three of them had founded the firm together. More than that, they'd been Ryan's most supportive friends.

She asked, "What on earth happened?"

Ryan shrugged and said in a reticent voice, "Something to do with my being a liability to the firm ... I don't know."

But Riley could tell by his caginess that he knew exactly why he was being forced out.

And it only took a moment for her to guess the reason.

"Sexual harassment," she said.

Ryan winced at the words.

"Look, it was all a misunderstanding," he said.

Riley almost had to bite her tongue to keep from saying ...

"Yeah, I'll bet it was."

Avoiding Riley's eyes, Ryan continued, "Her name is Kyanne, and she's an associate, and she's young ..."

As his voice trailed off for a moment, Riley thought ...

Of course she's young.

They're always young.

Ryan said, "And I thought everything was mutual. I really did. It started off with some flirtation—on both of our parts, believe me. Then it escalated from there until ... well, she went to Paul and Barrett complaining about a toxic work environment. They tried to handle it with a nondisclosure agreement, but she wouldn't settle. Nothing would do, I guess, except for me to go."

He fell quiet again, and Riley tried to grasp all that he was leaving unsaid. It wasn't hard to put together a possible scenario.

35

Ryan had gotten enthralled with a pretty and vivacious associate, maybe an ambitious young woman with her eye on an eventual partnership.

How far did Ryan go? she wondered.

She doubted that he would have held a promotion over her head in exchange for sexual favors ...

He's not that *kind of a creep,* she thought.

And maybe Ryan was also telling the truth about the attraction being mutual, at least at the start. Maybe they'd even had a consensual affair. But at some point things had soured, and the woman, Kyanne, hadn't liked what was happening between them.

Probably with good reason, Riley figured.

How could Kyanne have helped thinking that her future with the firm was somehow linked to her relationship with Ryan? He was a full partner, after all. He wielded the power in their relationship.

Still, something didn't add up for Riley ...

She said, "So Paul and Barrett are forcing you out? That's their solution?"

Ryan nodded, and Riley shook her head with disbelief.

Paul and Barrett weren't exactly Boy Scouts themselves, and Riley had overheard some pretty salacious talk among all three of the partners over the years. She was sure that their behavior had been no better than Ryan's—possibly considerably worse.

She said, "Ryan, you said she wouldn't sign an NDA."

Ryan nodded and took a sip of his drink.

Very cautiously she asked, "How many sexual harassment NDAs have you worked out over the years?"

Ryan winced again, and Riley knew she'd hit upon the truth.

She added, "And Paul and Barrett—how many NDAs have they had to negotiate for themselves?"

Ryan began, "Riley, I'd rather not get into—"

"No, of course you wouldn't," Riley interrupted. "Ryan, you're being scapegoated. You know that, don't you? Paul and Barrett are trying to clean up the firm's image, make it look like they've got some kind of zero-tolerance policy toward harassment. Getting rid of you is their way of doing that."

Ryan shrugged and said, "I know. But what can I do?"

Riley certainly didn't know what to tell him. She didn't want to sympathize with him. He'd been digging this hole for himself for years. Even so, she hated the trick his partners had played on him.

But she knew there was nothing he could do about it now. Besides, something else was worrying her.

Nodding toward the bags, she asked, "What are these for?"

Ryan looked at the bags for a moment.

Then he said in a choked voice, "Riley, I can't go home."

Riley gasped aloud.

"What do you mean?" she asked. "Did you lose the house?"

"No, not yet. It's just that …"

Ryan's voice faded, then he said …

"I can't face it alone. I can't live in that house alone. I keep remembering happy times with you and April. I keep thinking about how badly I screwed things up for all of us. The place breaks my heart, Riley."

He took out his handkerchief and wiped his eyes. Riley was shocked. She'd very rarely seen Ryan cry. She almost felt like crying herself.

But she knew she had a serious problem to solve right now.

She said in a gentle voice …

"Ryan, you can't stay here."

Ryan shriveled like a punctured balloon. Riley wished her words weren't so hurtful. But she had to be honest.

"I've got my own life now," she said. "I've got two girls to raise. And it's a good life. Blaine and I are serious about each other—really serious. In fact …"

She almost went on to tell him about Blaine's plans to build onto his house.

But no, that would be too much right now.

Instead she said, "You can sell our old house."

"I know," Ryan said, still crying softly. "I plan to. But in the meantime … I just can't live there."

Riley wished she could do something to comfort him—take his hand, give him a hug, or some other physical gesture of comfort.

It was tempting, and some of her old feeling for him was welling up inside her but …

Don't do it, she told herself.

Stay cool.

Think of Blaine.

Think of the kids.

Ryan was sobbing pathetically now. In a truly frantic voice he said …

"Riley, I'm sorry. I want to start all over. I want to be a good husband and a good dad. Surely I can do that if … we try again."

Still keeping physical space between them, Riley said …

"Ryan, we can't. It's way too late for that."

"It's never too late," Ryan cried. "Let's just go away, the two of us, put things back together."

Riley shuddered deeply.

He doesn't know what he's saying, she thought.

He's having a nervous breakdown.

She also felt pretty sure now that he'd been drinking earlier today.

Then, with a nervous laugh, he said …

"I've got it! Let's head up to your dad's cabin! I've never even been there, can you believe it? Not once in all these years. We can spend a few days there and—"

Riley interrupted him sharply, "Ryan no."

He stared at her as if he couldn't believe his ears.

In a gentler voice Riley said, "I've sold the cabin, Ryan. And even if I hadn't …"

She fell silent for a moment, then said …

"Ryan, you've got to pull yourself out of this. I wish I could help you, but I can't."

Ryan's shoulders sagged and his sobbing grew quieter. He seemed to be taking Riley's words to heart.

She said, "You're a tough, smart, resourceful man. You can come back from all this. I know you can. But I can't be a part of it. It wouldn't be good for me—and if you're honest with yourself, you know it wouldn't be good for you either."

Ryan nodded miserably.

"You're right," he said, his voice steadier now. "It's my own mess and I've got to fix it. I'm sorry I bothered you. I'll go home now."

As he got to his feet, Riley said …

"Wait a minute. You're in no condition to drive home. Let me drive you. You can come back and get your car when you're feeling better."

Ryan nodded again.

Riley was relieved that they weren't going to have an argument about it, and that she didn't have to forcibly take his car keys away from him.

Riley finally dared to take him by the arm as she led him out to her own car. He really did seem to need her physical support.

They were both silent during the drive. When they pulled up to the big, beautiful house they'd once shared, he said, "Riley, there's something I've been meaning to tell you. I ... I think you've done really well. And I wish you every happiness."

Riley felt a lump in her throat.

"Oh, Ryan—" she began.

"No, please listen to me, because this is important. I admire you. You've done so many great things. You've been a great mother to April, and you've adopted Jilly, and you're starting into a relationship, and I can tell that he's a great guy. And all the while you've been doing your job, stopping bad guys, saving lives. I don't know how you've done it. Your life is all of a piece."

Riley was deeply startled—and deeply disturbed.

When was the last time Ryan had said anything like this to her?

She simply had no idea what to say.

To her relief, Ryan got out of the car without saying another word.

Riley sat staring at the house as Ryan went on inside. Her heart really went out to him. She couldn't imagine facing that house alone herself—not with all the memories it harbored, both good or bad.

And those words he'd said ...

"Your life is all of a piece."

She sighed and murmured aloud ...

"It's not true."

It was still a struggle for her, raising two girls while working at a consuming and often dangerous job. She was pulled in too many directions, had too many commitments, and she hadn't yet learned to handle it.

Was it always going to be this way?

And how was Blaine going to fit into it all?

Was a successful marriage even possible for her?

She shuddered at the thought that maybe she'd be in Ryan's shoes one day.

Then she pulled away from the house where she had once lived, and drove back home.

CHAPTER EIGHT

Riley was pacing the floor in her living room.

She told herself that she should just relax now, that she'd learned all about relaxing on her recent vacation. But when she thought about that, she found herself remembering what her father had said in her nightmare …

"You're a hunter, like me."

But she sure didn't feel like a hunter at the moment.

More like a caged animal, she thought.

She'd just gotten home from taking the girls to their first day of school. Jilly was delighted to finally be in the same high school as her sister. The new students and their parents got the customary welcome in the auditorium, then a quick tour of the students' classrooms. April had been able to join Riley and Jilly for the tour.

Although Riley hadn't had a chance to talk at length with each teacher, she'd managed to say hello and introduce herself as Jilly's mother and April as Jilly's sister. Some of Jilly's new teachers had taught April in earlier years, and they had nice things to say about her.

When Riley had wanted to hang around after the orientation, both girls had teased her.

"And do what?" April had asked. *"Go to all of Jilly's classes?"*

Riley had said maybe she would, provoking a moan of despair from Jilly.

"Mo-o-o-m! That would be so uncool!"

April had laughed and said, *"Mom, don't be a chopper."*

When Riley asked what a "chopper" was, April informed her it meant "helicopter parent."

One of those terms I ought to be up on, Riley thought.

Anyway, Riley had respected Jilly's pride and come on home—and now here she was. Gabriela had gone out to meet one of her numerous cousins for lunch, then do some grocery shopping. So Riley was alone in the house, except for a dog and a cat that didn't seem the least bit interested in her.

I've got to snap out of this, she thought.

Riley went to the kitchen and got herself a snack. Then she forced herself to sit down in the living room and turned on the TV. The news was depressing, so she switched to a daytime soap. She had no idea what was going on in the story, but it was diverting, at least for a little while.

But her attention soon wandered, and she found herself thinking about what Ryan had said during his awful visit when she got back from the beach …

"I can't face it alone. I can't live in that house alone."

Right now, Riley had some idea of how he felt.

Were she and her ex-husband more alike than she wanted to admit?

She tried to convince herself otherwise. Unlike Ryan, she was taking care of her family. Later today, the girls and Gabriela would all be home and they'd have dinner together. Maybe this weekend Blaine and Crystal would join them.

That thought reminded Riley that Blaine had been a little bit reserved toward her ever since the whole thing with Ryan had happened. Riley could understand why. Riley hadn't wanted to talk to Blaine about the visit afterward—it seemed too intimate and personal—and it was only natural that Blaine had felt uncomfortable about it.

She had an urge to phone him right now, but she knew that Blaine was putting in a lot of hours catching up with things at his restaurant now that their vacation was over.

So now here Riley was, feeling terribly alone in her own house …

Just like Ryan.

She couldn't help feeling a little guilty toward her ex-husband—although she couldn't imagine why. Nothing that was wrong in his life was her fault. Even so, she more than half-wanted to give him a call, find out how he was doing, maybe commiserate with him a little. But of course, that was an incredibly stupid idea. The last thing she wanted to do was give him any false signals that they might get together again.

As the soap opera characters argued, wept, slapped each other, and jumped in out of bed with each other, something occurred to Riley.

Sometimes her own life at home, her family and relationships, didn't seem any more real to her than what she was watching on TV. The actual presence of her loved ones tended to distract her from her deep-seated sense of isolation. But even just a few hours by herself in the house was enough to painfully remind her of how truly alone she felt inside.

There was an empty place inside her that could only be filled by …

What, exactly?

By work.

But how meaningful was her work, to herself or to anybody else?

Again she remembered something her father had said in that dream …

"It's a damn crazy useless life you've got—seeking justice for people who're already dead, exactly the people who don't need justice anymore."

She wondered …

Is that true?

Is what I do really useless?

Surely not, since she often stopped killers who would certainly have killed again if they could have.

She saved lives in the long run—just how many lives, she couldn't begin to imagine.

And yet, in order for her to even have a job to do, *somebody* had to kill, and *somebody* had to die …

It always starts with death.

And more often than not, her cases continued to nag at her and haunt her even after they were solved, after the killers were slain or brought to justice.

She turned off the television, which was only irritating her now. Then she sat back and closed her eyes and thought about her most recent case, that of a serial killer down in Georgia.

Poor Morgan, she thought.

Morgan Farrell had been married to a wealthy but abusive man. When he'd been brutally stabbed to death in his sleep, Morgan had been sure she was the one who had killed him, even though she couldn't remember the deed.

She was sure she'd forgotten about it because of pills and alcohol.

And she'd been proud of what she'd thought she'd done. She'd even called Riley by phone to tell her so …

"I killed the bastard."

Morgan had been innocent, as things turned out. Another

deranged woman had killed Morgan's husband—and several other equally abusive husbands.

The woman, who had suffered at her own late husband's hands, had been on a vigilante mission to free other women from that pain. Riley had stopped her just before she could mistakenly kill a man who wasn't guilty of anything except loving his disturbed, delusional wife.

Riley replayed the scene in her mind, after she'd fought the woman to the ground and was putting her in handcuffs …

"Adrienne McKinney, you're under arrest."

But now Riley wondered …

What if everything could have ended differently?

What if Riley been able to save the innocent man, explain to the woman the mistake she'd made, and then simply let her go?

She'd have kept on killing, Riley thought.

And the men she killed would have deserved to die.

So what kind of justice had she really carried out that time?

Riley's heart sank, and she remembered again her father's words …

"It's a damn crazy useless life you've got."

On one hand, she was desperately trying to live the life of a mother raising two daughters, the life of a woman in love with a man she hoped to marry. At times, that life seemed to be actually working out for her, and she knew she would never stop trying to be good at it.

But as soon as she found herself alone, that ordinary life seemed unreal.

On the other hand, she struggled against awful odds to bring down monsters. Her work was intensely important to her, even though it all too often began and ended in pure futility.

Riley felt perfectly miserable now. Despite the early hour, she was tempted to pour herself a stiff drink. As she resisted that temptation, her phone rang. When she saw who the caller was, she breathed a huge sigh of relief.

This was real.

She had work to do.

CHAPTER NINE

During her drive to the BAU building, Riley realized that her feelings were mixed about getting back to work. When Meredith had called her, she'd known by his tone of voice that he wasn't in a good mood.

He hadn't offered any details. He'd just said that he was calling a meeting of her team about some new developments. She'd been relieved to get out of the house and head for Quantico. Now she found herself wondering what Meredith was mad about.

About a week and a half ago, he had suggested that she go down to Rushville, Mississippi, to check on a murder that had just happened there. Riley had told him no.

But he hadn't seemed angry with her then. In fact, he'd been downright apologetic for bothering her.

"I'm sorry I bothered you," he'd said. *"Keep on enjoying your vacation."*

Something had changed since then.

Whatever that change was, it probably meant that she had real work to do. Riley's spirits lifted as she pulled up in front of the big white building that held the Behavioral Analysis Unit. She realized that it felt like coming home.

After she parked her car, Riley opened the trunk and took out her go-bag, which she kept always ready. She knew it was likely that she was about to head out on a new case.

When she walked into the conference room, the meeting was just getting underway. Riley's two partners, Bill Jeffreys and Jenn Roston, were sitting across the table from Special Agent Brent Meredith, the team chief.

As always, Meredith cut a daunting figure, with his big frame and his black, angular features.

But today he looked more intimidating than usual. He glowered at Riley as she took a seat at the table.

Then he snapped, "How was your vacation, Agent Paige?"

His sharp words cut Riley. Instead of responding to Meredith's question, she returned his gaze and said firmly, "I'm ready to get back to work."

Meredith nodded with sullen approval.

Then he said, "Now that we're all here, let's get started."

Glancing among his three colleagues, Meredith added, "I kept thinking about the murder down in Rushville, Mississippi—the one the local cop there called us about. I asked Agent Jeffreys here to do a little research on it. He did, and now he's thinking maybe we should look into it after all. Would you care to explain, Agent Jeffreys?"

"Certainly," Bill said as he stood up walked over to the screen in front of the room. Bill had been Riley's partner and close friend for many years, and Riley was happy to see him here. He was about her age, a solid, striking man with touches of gray in his dark hair.

Bill clicked a remote and a couple of images appeared on the screen. One was of a taciturn-looking man in his fifties. The other was of the same man's corpse stretched out on hardwood floor with a single brutal deep, roundish wound in his forehead.

Pointing to the images, Bill explained …

"Gareth Ogden was killed in his home in Rushville eleven days ago. The murder took place at about eight-thirty in the evening. He was killed by a single hammer blow to the forehead."

Looking at Riley and Jenn, Meredith added, "This was the murder that the local cop there called the BAU about. She was very insistent, and I wound up talking to her myself. She was concerned about the resemblance of Ogden's killing to the unsolved murders of an entire family that happened in Rushville some ten years ago."

"That's right," Bill said. "I started looking into it, and this is what I found."

Bill clicked the remote again, and a new set of images came up. A man and a woman lay in a blood-drenched bed, their skulls literally pulverized. The other two victims, killed in an identical manner, lay in their own beds—one a teenaged boy, and the other a girl who looked about ten or twelve years old.

Bill explained …

"While the Bonnett family lay asleep, an intruder crept into their home. First he bludgeoned the daughter, Lisa, to death in her bedroom. After that he crept to the room where her brother, Martin, lay asleep, and killed him too. Finally, he made his way to the parents' bedroom. He bashed Leona Bonnett's head in while she slept. Her husband, Cosmo, appears to have been awakened, and a brief struggle ensued before he became the final victim."

Jenn Roston squinted at the screen and said, "It's shocking, sure. But if there's a connection between the murder of the family and Ogden's death, I'm not sure I see it—aside from the weapon used."

Riley nodded in approval. Jenn was a young African-American woman who had already proven herself to be a remarkably capable agent during her short time at the BAU. Riley and Jenn had worked together on several cases. Their relationship had been rocky at first but a lot of trust had soon grown between them.

Meredith said, "Explain, Agent Roston."

Jenn pointed to the grisly images on the screen and said, "The Bonnett murders were remarkably brutal. It looks like each of their heads was repeatedly bashed, blow after blow. The killings were clearly carried out in a rage, for deeply personal reasons. Agent Jeffreys, could you show us those other pictures again?"

Bill clicked the remote, and the pictures of Ogden appeared.

Jenn pointed to the photo of his dead body and said, "Ogden's murder was swift and clean by comparison. He died from what looked like a single hammer blow to the forehead. No rage was involved. His killing seems coldblooded and ... what's the word I'm looking for? Almost surgical."

Riley was intrigued, and what Jenn was saying made sense to her.

"Yes, and murders with a hammer are actually pretty common," Riley said. "It could be just a coincidence."

Meredith asked Bill, "How big a town is Rushville?"

Bill said, "It's just a little town on the Gulf coast, with a population of about sixty-five hundred. That's part of what bothers me. They normally get virtually no violent crime there—just some aggravated assaults, burglary and thefts, and stolen cars. So if it *is* a coincidence, it's a pretty weird one—a new murder committed with a hammer in a town like that, even after a long period of time."

Jenn scratched her chin and said, "So what are you thinking— that a single killer has been dormant all this time? Isn't that kind of a stretch?"

"Not really," Bill said. "Are you familiar with the so-called BTK killer?"

Jenn shook her head no.

Of course, Riley knew what killer Bill was referring to, and she was interested in hearing what point he intended to make.

Bill brought up some more pictures showing the BTK killer's bound, beaten, and strangled victims.

He said, "Dennis Rader was a classic psychopath—outwardly charming, a Scout Master and a president of his church congregation. But his murders were so brutal that he called himself the BTK killer—the initials meant 'bind, torture, and kill.' He killed four members of one family in 1988, then a single female the same year."

Meredith added, "Then he vanished for three years before he killed again. He kept going dormant between his ten murders, sometimes going longer than five years with no activity."

"That's right," Bill said. "During his active years he sent taunting letters to the media. Then he completely disappeared for ten years. He started sending letters again in 2004, and that led to his arrest and conviction in 2005, more than forty years after he'd started killing."

Bill paused, seeming to wait for some response.

Meredith wrinkled his brow and said, "I see some similarities, but also some differences. If there's a serial killer in Rushville, he's not a publicity seeker. Remember, the BTK killer positively craved publicity, and he'd get quite irate when he didn't get enough attention. Some of the photos you're showing were taken by him and sent out to the media, along with crime scene souvenirs."

Riley said to Bill, "Still, I see what you're getting at. Not only did the BTK killer stay dormant for years at a time, but his MO changed. He started out as a classic 'family annihilator,' then changed to single serial victims. Maybe Rushville has got the same kind of killer."

Bill nodded and said, "If so, those ten years between murders was just an unusually long cooling off period. The original murders might have been in rage, but maybe the guy found that he enjoyed it. Maybe he's spent a long time thinking about how he could repeat it. We just don't know what's going on in that town, and I'd rather not take a chance on a thing like this never happening again."

Riley studied her colleagues' faces. Jenn still looked skeptical, but Riley sensed that Meredith agreed with Bill.

Riley asked Meredith, "Did the FBI get involved with the unsolved Bonnett killings?"

Meredith growled a little.

"No, the local cops tried to handle it until the case went cold," he said. "And that might be a problem. When I talked to Carter Crane, the police chief down in Rushville, he insisted there was no connection at all. He was actually kind of defensive about it, and mad at the cop who called us about it. The chances of him *asking* for the FBI's help are just about nil."

Meredith drummed his fingers on the table for a moment.

Then he said, "Aw, to hell with it. We actually were asked to get involved by a police officer from Rushville, the young one who called—Samantha Kuehling is her name. I want you three to go down there anyway, and I'll get a plane ready ASAP. When you get there talk to Crane personally, try to convince him that he might have a serious problem on his hands, and that he really needs our help. I'll call ahead to give him a heads-up. Don't expect a cozy welcome, though."

As the meeting broke up, Riley felt newly energized—even better than she'd felt when she'd been enjoying her vacation.

What does that say about me? she wondered.

Was she more at home among the world's monsters than among the people she loved?

She remembered again those words her father had said in that dream and also while he was still alive …

"You're a hunter, like me."

She sighed and thought …

At least I don't feel like I'm in a cage anymore.

She called Gabriela to let her and the kids know she was on her way to Mississippi.

CHAPTER TEN

Riley flinched at the hot blast of air as she, Bill, and Jenn got out of the car in front of the Rushville police station.

She wondered …

Is it always this hot here this time of year?

The heat had actually been worse on the scorching tarmac when they got off the BAU plane in Biloxi. It had felt like walking into a steam room. Agents from the nearby FBI resident agency had met them at the plane, turned over a vehicle for their use, scurried back into their own car with its air conditioning still running, and driven away without further to-do.

Riley fanned herself with her free hand as they walked toward the small, plain, red brick police station.

Summers could be hot in Virginia, but Riley couldn't remember experiencing this kind of oppressive, humid heat there. She noticed that the pedestrians on the nearby sidewalk were moving slowly, like characters in some horror movie about people being under a spell or replaced by automaton-like aliens.

They clearly didn't like the weather very much either.

At yet Riley wondered …

Does anybody in this town like much of anything?

As soon as they'd driven into town, she'd realized that Rushville felt and looked curiously dead and demoralized.

Riley was relieved to feel air conditioning as they walked on inside. She and her colleagues found themselves in a large open area with a bunch of desks. About eight or nine uniformed cops were sitting at their desks or wandering around—all of them male except for one small but formidable-looking short-haired woman, who appeared to be the youngest.

Is that Samantha Kuehling? Riley wondered.

In the front of the area, a grim-looking secretary sat at her desk doing her nails.

Upon seeing the new arrivals, the woman touched her intercom and mumbled something inaudible.

Immediately a uniformed man strode out of the office behind her—the police chief, Riley realized. He looked a little young for his job, and Riley sensed right away that he was defensive about it.

Riley and her colleagues took out their badges and introduced themselves.

The man crossed his arms and said, "I know who the hell you are."

Ignoring Riley and Jenn and talking directly to Bill, he said …

"I'm Carter Crane, and I'm in charge here—or at least I like to think so. I'll just tell you what I told your boss, Agent Meredith. You've wasted taxpayer money on a pointless trip, and you might as well drive back to Biloxi and fly on back to Quantico. You've got no business here."

Beaming with triumph and obviously pleased with himself for putting three FBI agents in their place, he looked around at the cops in the room. Then he turned around walked back toward his office.

Bill said in a sharp, clear, but polite voice, "Chief Crane, please just give us a few minutes of your time."

Crane turned around and looked at the three agents indecisively. He didn't seem to know what else to say to exert his authority.

Not quite the "big dog" he wants to be, Riley thought.

Now Crane glanced around at the cops in the room a bit sheepishly.

With a soft growl he said, "Come on into my office."

Bill made a move as if to follow him, but Riley touched his shoulder, stopping him.

Let's not make this easy on the guy, she thought.

Crane seemed to her like the kind of man who deserved to be embarrassed in front of his team …

It might even be good for him.

She said, "Oh, no need for that, Chief Crane. I'm sure we can talk things over right here."

Chief Crane gave her a startled look. Riley noticed a slight grin on Bill's face. He obviously understood and approved of Riley's gambit.

"OK, but make this quick," Crane said, hunching over a little and shuffling his feet uneasily. "I'm in the middle of a busy day here."

Bill said, "We understand that you had a murder here about a week and a half ago. A certain Gareth Ogden was the victim."

Crane nodded.

Bill added, "And we understand that his murder bears some

resemblance to a family annihilation that took place here about ten years ago—the mass murder of the Bonnett family."

Crane was looking more and more uncomfortable. Meanwhile, the cops who were standing or sitting around them were gawking with curiosity—all except the young woman, who was smiling.

Yeah, that must be Samantha Kuehling, Riley thought.

The chief barked with nervous anger, "Look, there's really nothing to all this. Aside from the use of a hammer as a murder weapon, there's no resemblance at all between the crimes. The Bonnett family case went cold years ago, and we'll probably never know who did it. This new murder was obviously committed by some drifter who came and went."

"That might be so," Bill said. "But we'd like to share some of our thoughts about it."

As Bill started to explain the possible similarities to the BTK killer, Riley scanned the faces of the cops around her. She noticed all of them except the young woman were eyeing herself and Jenn somewhat warily.

Riley quickly realized that she was now in the Deep South, with all of its attitudes and bigotries …

Jenn and I are both women.

And Jenn's black.

Crane kept sighing irritably and rolling his eyes as Bill went on explaining his theory, including the possible relevance of the BTK killer. It was obvious to Riley that Crane was determined not to believe anything Bill said.

Finally Bill told him …

"So you can see, all we want to do is make sure you don't have a serious problem here."

Crane scoffed, and his voice shook with anger.

"Oh, so *that's* all you want."

Crane looked around at the cops in the room.

"Hear that, guys?" he barked. "These goddamn Feds are here out of the goodness of their hearts."

Most of the men chuckled cynically in solidarity with their chief—but not the woman, Riley noticed.

Riley felt a flash of discouragement. The way things were going, she and her colleagues were liable to have to fly back to Quantico today after all.

Riley thought fast about how to turn this situation around in their favor.

She remembered something Meredith had said to her during their phone call when she'd been on vacation—something Crane had told him about Samantha Kuehling ...

"Just some bored small-town cop looking for excitement."

She also remembered what Meredith had said during their meeting this morning—that Crane was *"mad at the cop who called us about it."*

Riley smiled to herself.

Now she knew exactly how to really push Crane's buttons—and maybe even change how he was dealing with them.

She looked over at the woman sitting at her desk and called out ...

"What are your thoughts about this, Officer Kuehling?"

The woman's eyes widened at the sound of her name. Riley was relieved that she'd correctly guessed her identity.

Picking up his cue to go along with Riley's tactic, Bill said to the woman ...

"Yeah, come on over here, Officer Kuehling. Talk to us about it. Give us your opinion."

Looking both embarrassed and thrilled, Kuehling got up from her desk and walked toward them.

The male cops looked thoroughly dumbfounded now—but none of them more so than Chief Crane. Riley could well understand why. Not only had Riley and her colleagues known the name of the only woman on his force, but they were more interested in her thoughts than they were in his own.

When Kuehling joined the group, Bill asked her, "What can you tell us about Gareth Ogden's murder?"

Kuehling shrugged a little and said, "Well, quite a lot, actually."

She pointed to a youngish man who was still sitting on the opposite side of her desk, looking as nonplussed as the rest of the men.

"My partner, Officer Wolfe—he and I were the first on the scene that morning. We'd just gotten a call from a local paperboy who'd found the body."

Riley nodded, silently encouraging Kuehling to continue.

Kuehling said, "Well, Dominic—Officer Wolfe—thought right away that the killer was some drifter who had come and gone."

Riley said, "So goes the prevailing theory, it seems. Why do you think differently?"

Kuehling's brow wrinkled with thought.

"I guess it was the murder weapon, mostly. I could tell by the size and shape of the wound that it was either a claw hammer or a rip hammer. One of the first things I did was check the victim's tool chest. And his whole set of hammers was hanging there, looking as clean as a whistle."

Riley was already impressed by Kuehling's methods and her powers of observation.

"And there was no other weapon left at the scene?" Riley asked.

"No, there wasn't," Kuehling said. "So the killer took it with him when he left. Maybe he threw it away afterwards, but I somehow doubt it. More important, he *showed up* there with the hammer. Doesn't that suggest premeditation? I mean, what kind of a drifter wanders around carrying a hammer everywhere he goes? It just doesn't make sense to me."

Riley asked, "Was there any evidence of robbery?"

"None that I could see," Kuehling said. "The chief still thinks robbery might have been a motive, like maybe the killer took some money Ogden left lying around that we don't know about. But …"

She hesitated, seeming a bit unsure about whether she really dared to directly contradict her boss.

Then she said, "Why wouldn't he have stolen anything else in the house? He didn't even take Ogden's wallet. I don't get it."

Bill said, "So you're worried the culprit isn't through killing?"

"That's right, I don't think he is," Kuehling said, sounding more and more self-confident. "And I think he lives right here in Rushville—and he's probably somebody everybody knows. And I think …"

Her voice faded for a moment.

Then she said quietly, "I think he also killed the Bonnett family ten years ago. Agent Jeffreys, what you said right now about the BTK killer makes sense to me. I think our killer is like that. He's been thinking about the Bonnetts all these years, and he's been wanting to do something like that again this whole time. Something in him finally snapped, and he took another victim's life, and he isn't through yet. He won't be through until we stop him."

Kuehling's voice was starting to tremble with emotion.

"I'll admit, I'm not completely objective about this. My dad was a cop here when the Bonnett family got killed, and he never got over not solving it. It's been one of the biggest regrets of his life. I

53

wish I could make things right for him."

One of the older cops nodded his head and said ...

"Yeah, I was on the force back then too, and I feel the same way as old Art Kuehling. The Bonnetts were good folks, and they deserved justice then, and they still do. I hate the fact that the case went cold. The thought that their killer is still living right around here ... well, it's been eating me up inside for a long time."

There was a murmur of interest in the room, especially from the older cops.

Kuehling looked directly at Riley and said ...

"Look, maybe the chief's right and there's no connection between Ogden's killing and what happened to the Bonnetts. But shouldn't we at least check it out? Maybe if nothing else, we could finally solve the Bonnett case. But we won't be able to do that on our own. We need the FBI's help."

Kuehling gulped hard and added ...

"And I for one am really glad you're here."

One of the cops said loudly ...

"Well said, Sam. I'm glad they're here too."

Now there was a chorus of agreement among the cops.

Riley was pleased that the tide of opinion seemed to be moving their way. Even so, she saw that not everyone was ready to take their side.

Crane's face was red and twisted with embarrassment and anger.

"OK, then," he said. "I'll give you Feds a chance to see what you can do. I'll be pretty damned surprised if you find anything. I can't spare you any personnel to speak of. But you can take Kuehling if you think she'll be any good to you. And her partner too."

Then Crane turned and looked at the other cops and said, "What are you guys gawking for? Get back to work."

The men grumbled a little as they did as they were told, and Crane walked sullenly back into his office and shut the door behind him.

Officer Kuehling stood there with her mouth hanging open with amazement.

Riley said to her, "Well, let's get going."

Then Riley looked over at Kuehling's partner, the young man with a dumbfounded look who was standing at his desk.

Riley said to him, "And you too. We should get a look at the scene of Ogden's murder."

"OK," Kuehling said. "Officer Wolfe and I will drive ahead and show you the way."

As Kuehling and Wolfe followed Riley and her colleagues through the station, Jenn nudged Riley and said with a chuckle, "That chief is pretty pissed off. I swear to God, Riley, I've never met anyone who can make enemies faster than you. Congratulations."

Riley laughed and said, "Thanks."

She had to admit to herself, she'd enjoyed putting Chief Crane in his place.

I just hope it doesn't backfire on me, she thought.

CHAPTER ELEVEN

Riley admired the wide sand and calm Gulf waters as Bill drove the FBI car along the beachfront road. But her spirits sank when the police car they were following pulled up to the house they wanted to check out.

"Looks like we got here just in time," Jenn said from the back seat.

A moving van was parked in front of the weather-beaten house, and a "FOR SALE" sign was fastened to the flight of steps leading up to the high porch. The van was fairly stuffed with furniture, and Riley guessed that the movers must be almost finished with their job.

Officers Kuehling and Wolfe got out of the police car and stood waiting for the three agents to join them.

As Bill parked the car and they all got out, Riley grumbled, "I didn't figure on finding the crime scene intact. But I didn't expect to find the whole place damn near empty."

Bill chuckled a little and said, "Don't worry. If the killer left any vibes in there, you'll pick them up anyway."

Riley fought down a sigh.

After all, getting into killers' minds was what Riley was known for, but there were no guarantees about that happening. Her talent could be erratic.

When Riley and her two colleagues got out of the car, even the nearby surf didn't offer any relief against the heat. They followed Kuehling and Wolfe up the front stairs. The three of them squeezed against the banister as a couple of movers lugged a dining room cupboard down toward the moving van.

When they crossed the broad porch and walked inside the house through the open door, they found themselves in a completely barren living room.

Samantha Kuehling pointed to the floor. "That was where we found him lying on his back."

Riley looked at the hardwood floor. She remembered seeing quite a bit of blood in the crime scene photo, but none was left here now. She could see where the boards had been carefully scrubbed, sanded, and refinished.

Of course she wasn't surprised. The murder had taken place well over a week ago. The police had long since finished examining the crime scene, and naturally, whoever owned the house had wanted to clean it up.

There was quite a bit of thumping and banging in the adjoining dining room. Riley glanced through the arched doorway and saw a stout woman about her own age giving orders to a pair of movers. The men were preparing to take out an empty glass-enclosed curio cabinet.

The woman turned and saw the new arrivals and asked, "Can I help you? Are you here to look at the house?"

Then noticing Officer Kuehling she added with a note of disappointment, "Oh, it's you again. More cop stuff, I guess. Well, I'll try to help however I can."

The woman came into the living room and Kuehling introduced her as Cathy Lilly, Gareth Ogden's married daughter who lived in Jacksonville.

Cathy wiped her sweating brow with a handkerchief and said …

"Well, I wish I could offer you a place to sit or maybe something cool to drink on a miserable day like this, but as you can see, everything is pretty much gone."

Riley noted that the woman was wearing sneakers and cut-off jeans and a T-shirt, and she was also wearing an ornate necklace. It was a silver pendant decorated with small diamonds.

Although that seemed a bit incongruous, Riley decided to ease into her questions with some idle conversation.

"Are you having any luck selling the place?" she asked Cathy Lilly.

"I don't know yet," Cathy said. "Amos Crites, who owns the houses on either side of this one, is thinking about buying, but he's dillydallying around about things."

Then with a chuckle she added …

"I don't suppose I could interest any of you FBI folks in a beachfront house right here in beautiful Rushville, Mississippi? No, of course not. The property here's been damn near worthless since the hurricane, and it wasn't worth a hell of a lot even before then. As for all the furniture and stuff, I've managed to sell some of it, but a whole lot of it's going to go in storage. I don't know what I'll wind up doing with it."

She shuffled her feet a little and said, "I sure hope you can find who killed Dad. I've already answered a lot of police questions, but I don't mind going through it all again. The truth is, I don't know a hell of a lot about who might have wanted Daddy dead or why."

"Oh?" Riley said.

Office Kuehling explained, "Cathy didn't have a lot of contact with her father during the last few years."

Cathy nodded, and she sniffed sadly.

She said, "Dad got awfully hard to get along with after Mom died of ovarian cancer some twelve years ago. He just wasn't himself anymore, and he didn't like seeing me and my husband and our kids. I think it was just because we're happy, and seeing us reminded him of when Mom was alive and he was happy too, and that made him sad. So I just respected his wishes and stayed away pretty much."

Riley again noticed the pendant hanging around Cathy's neck. Again it struck her as a little odd, considering how casually the woman was dressed.

"That's a nice piece of jewelry," Riley said, looking at the pendant.

Cathy fingered it as if she'd forgotten she was wearing it.

"This? Oh, thanks. It belonged to my mom. I just found it lying around here when I showed up. I guess Dad liked to keep it where he could see it to remind him of Mom."

She lifted it a little for Riley to see and added, "See, he even kept it all polished up."

A banging sound from upstairs interrupted their conversation.

Cathy shrugged and said, "I guess I'd better check and see how the guys are doing up there. I hope you'll excuse me. If you need me, just give me a yell."

She trotted up the stairs, leaving the three agents and the two local cops in the living room. Riley looked around the sparkling clean, barren room, wondering how she was going to get an impression of the crime scene.

She asked Kuehling and Wolfe, "How well can you describe how things looked here when you found the body?"

Wolfe chuckled and said, "Oh, Sam can tell you all about that, believe me."

Samantha Kuehling immediately started walking slowly around the room, describing where everything had been. She recited the placement of every piece of furniture, the throw rugs on the floor, and even little items and knickknacks. She included a stray package of cigarettes and family photos that had been placed on furniture or that had been hanging from the walls.

She was even able to describe the furniture in detail—all the materials and colors, and that the couch was old and the stuffing was coming out in a few places, and that the armchair had been a recliner.

Then Kuehling added …

"Oh—and that necklace Cathy was wearing—it was lying on the side table under a lamp, right next to the armchair. I guess Cathy was right—he liked keeping it close by."

Riley was almost dumbstruck by all this detail. But then, she remembered how Kuehling had been able to identify the murder weapon as either a claw or a rip hammer just from looking at the dead man's wound.

She said to Kuehling, "You've got some pretty impressive powers of observation."

Wolfe laughed and said, "Doesn't she, though?"

Kuehling shrugged modestly and said, "Thanks. So people tell me. I'm not sure what it's good for, though."

Riley smiled and said, "Oh, it's good for a lot, believe me."

Riley closed her eyes and took a few long, deep breaths.

She heard Wolfe ask, "Uh—what are you doing?"

"Shh," Riley heard Jenn Roston say.

"Let her do her thing," Bill added in a quiet voice.

As Riley kept breathing, her earlier doubts dissipated, and she began to feel the strange touch of another presence …

The killer's mind.

CHAPTER TWELVE

Keeping her eyes closed, Riley turned slowly around. In her mind, the details that Officer Kuehling had described fell into place. She found that she could visualize the room as it had been that night.

Now she needed to sense what had unfolded here.

It was about eight-thirty in the evening, she reminded herself.

That meant it was getting pretty dark outside.

But what about in here?

It depended on whether Ogden had had the overhead light on, or just the table lamp that Kuehling had said was beside his chair.

Riley thought about the melancholy widower, his reluctance to even spend time with his own family.

He didn't like bright light in the house, she felt.

So the table lamp had possibly been the only light in the room.

With the room in full focus now, Riley opened her eyes, keeping all the details in her head.

She asked Kuehling and Wolfe, "How did the killer get in here?"

Kuehling shrugged and said, "He just walked in."

Dominic added, "Ogden generally left his front door wide open at night, especially when it was hot like this. That's not unusual in this town."

Riley thought for a moment, then asked …

"Does anybody have any idea what Ogden might have been doing just before he was killed?"

"Maybe so," Kuehling said. "I went down to the beach and there were some recent footprints in the sand above the tide line. Of course they didn't show any detail, but it looked like someone had walked right across from here down toward the surf and then back up across the road. There aren't a lot of people around here these days. My guess is that he walked outside and down on the beach, then came back up to his house where the killer was waiting for him."

Riley tilted her head with admiration.

That's pretty good deduction, she thought.

This young woman clearly had the makings of an exceptional

cop.

Riley swung open the screen door and walked out onto the porch. She looked across the beach and imagined what Gareth Ogden would have looked like, standing in the dim light at the water's edge and staring sadly out over the Gulf.

Because of the distance and the darkness and the sound of the surf, the killer could have crept up the stairs and into the house without worrying that Ogden would notice him.

He knew Ogden, she realized. *He was familiar with Ogden's habits.*

Riley imagined the weight of a hammer in her hand. She felt a smirk forming on her face as she sensed the killer's glee …

This is going to be easy.

Continuing to play out the killer's musings as she stared out over the water, Riley thought …

Ogden'll be turning back soon.

I need to get inside now.

I need to get myself ready.

She turned and walked back inside the house, ignoring the presence of Jenn, Bill, and the two local cops as they stood and watched her. She looked around the room, which didn't seem empty at all anymore. She could see everything in vivid detail, especially …

The pendant.

She stood looking down at where the side table had been, picturing the pendant necklace lying there, glittering under the lamp.

Just as the killer might well have done, she reached for it.

She pantomimed picking it up and looking at it, again playing out the killer's thoughts …

Pretty.

Probably worth something too.

Again Riley felt that smirk on her face, thinking what he might have told himself …

It's not what I'm here for, though.

I'm no common burglar.

… and she set the pendant back down.

Then Riley could feel the killer's adrenaline surge at the sounds of Ogden mounting the steps outside.

She felt his body brace in preparation as he turned toward the door. At the same time she flashed back to the images she'd seen of the slain Bonnett family, and how their skulls had been caved in with numerous hammer blows.

She shuddered slightly as she sensed the killer's thoughts …

This won't be like last time.

Not so sloppy and reckless.

Again, she imagined the weight of the hammer in her hand. Perhaps, she considered, the killer had even been practicing his swing lately to hone his aim, hitting trees with the hammer, pretending he was hitting Ogden's skull, preparing to strike that single perfect blow.

And then …

She could see the screen door opening, and Ogden stepping inside.

She could imagine Ogden squinting with surprise as she realized …

I'm standing between him and the lamp.

The killer was just a shadowy figure to Ogden.

Given another couple of seconds, Ogden's eyes might have adjusted, and he could have seen the killer's face, but …

I won't give him a chance.

She lifted the imaginary hammer above her head and crashed it precisely in the middle of Ogden's forehead. She felt and heard the crunch of his skull breaking open, yanked the hammer back, and watched with grim satisfaction as Ogden stood for a few seconds with a stunned expression, then collapsed onto his back.

Riley found herself gasping for breath as the visualization ended.

That was vivid, she thought. *That was damned vivid.*

She staggered past Bill, Jenn, and the two cops out onto the porch. She leaned trembling against the railing and brought her breathing under control.

Her colleagues and the two cops came out onto the porch, and Bill asked …

"What did you get? What did you see?"

Riley took a long, slow breath and said …

"The killings are connected—the mass killing of the Bonnetts and Ogden's murder. The killer is happy with his new work. And …"

Riley sighed bitterly.

"And he's got a taste for killing. He'll do it again. And soon, I think."

CHAPTER THIRTEEN

As Riley leaned against the porch railing trying to regain her calm, she related her experience to Bill, Jenn, and the two local cops. Although she told them about the killer's movements, she knew that they could never understand the intensity of her connection with his mind.

Finally she said, "The pendant's probably the most important thing. The killer just left it there on the table. If he were just some drifter, he'd never have done that. He'd have stolen it for sure. Officer Kuehling, you were right. Robbery wasn't the motive. I think the killer knew the victim, and he picked him out well in advance."

By now Officers Kuehling and Wolfe were staring at her with perplexity.

"What just happened?" Wolfe asked.

Jenn explained, "Agent Paige is known for her ability to get into a killer's mind."

Kuehling's eyes widened.

"Is that what you did just now?" the young woman asked. "You felt and saw everything the killer felt and saw when he murdered Mr. Ogden? And you knew what he was thinking? How do you do that? Is it like ESP or something?"

Riley fought down a sigh.

"No, it's nothing like that," she said. The experience had drained her, and she didn't feel like explaining her process.

Fortunately, Jenn spoke up.

"It's not paranormal or anything like that. It's just instinct. Agent Paige has got one-in-a-million instincts."

Kuehling seemed to be getting more excited by the second.

"Wow, what an incredible gift!" she said. "I mean, it must make it amazingly easy to solve murder cases."

Riley shook her head. "I wish that were true. It's not an exact science. In fact, it's not a science at all. It's really just ... well, kind of really intense *guessing,* I think you could say."

Bill chuckled and added, "But Agent Paige's guesses are better than almost anybody else's hard-thought reasoning and deduction."

Riley looked at Bill and said, "Yeah, well—don't forget, I get things wrong once in a while. I might be wrong this time. I mean, for all any of us really know, Chief Crane is right and the killer really was some random drifter."

But as she said so, she admitted to herself ...

I really don't think so.

Not now.

Her thoughts were distracted by banging and sharp voices coming from one of the houses next door to this one. She walked along the porch to that side, and saw that a pickup truck had parked in front of that house. A ladder now led up to the roof, where three workmen were replacing shingles. At the bottom of the ladder, a rotund man was yelling profanity-laced orders up to them. The men on the roof were answering him with their own cheerful insults.

Cathy Lilly came out through the screen door onto the porch. She walked over beside Riley and called out to the man on the ground ...

"Hey, Amos—when are you going to make up your mind about buying this place?"

The man let out a rasping chuckle and yelled up to the men on the roof ...

"Y'hear that, boys? The little lady here wants to know when I'm gonna make a decision."

The men laughed as if they were in on some sort of joke.

Cathy snapped at the man on the ground, "Don't go holding your breath for me to bring the price down."

All of the men laughed again.

"We'll see about that, sweetheart," the obese man said.

Cathy muttered under her breath, "I'm not your sweetheart, you redneck jerk."

Then the man turned back to his workman and yelled ...

"What's the matter with you lazy bastards? Get moving, why don't you?"

One of the men yelled back, "Get moving yourself, Crites!"

"Why don't you come up here and give us a hand?" another said.

The third said to his companions, "Crites could never get his fat ass up here. He'd bust the ladder to pieces if he tried."

The man on the ground snarled at the insult and yelled ...

"Don't forget who signs your checks, you good-for-nothing peckerwoods. I've got half a mind to replace you with some

64

Mexicans. They'll work a whole lot cheaper—and not a whole lot worse, I don't reckon."

The man watched as his team resumed their work.

Riley said to Cathy, "I take it that's the man you mentioned—the one who owns the houses on both sides of this one."

Cathy nodded and said, "Yep, that's Amos Crites. In a town full of jerks, he must be just about the nastiest. Well, that's enough of him for a while. I'd better get back inside, make sure things are going OK with the movers."

Riley thanked Cathy for her cooperation and gave her a card with her contact information. When Cathy went back into the house, Riley said to her colleagues and the two cops, "It's time we started doing some interviews. We might as well start with this Amos Crites guy."

Samantha Kuehling was beaming with delight now. Riley sensed that she was excited to be part of a real investigation. But her partner, Dominic Wolfe, still looked puzzled. He seemed to be having a hard time grasping what was going on.

They all walked down the stairs and over to the next house. As they approached Amos Crites, Riley, Bill, and Jenn produced their badges and introduced themselves.

Crites chuckled snidely.

"Feds, huh?" he said.

He looked directly at Jenn as if in disbelief, then laughed caustically.

Riley immediately understood his unspoken racism. The idea of an African-American working in Federal-level law enforcement clearly amused him, and he wanted everybody to know it.

Riley could see Jenn clench her fists as she struggled to keep quiet.

The man's laughter died down and he said, "Well, I guess Gareth Ogden's daughter told you all about me."

"Not really," Riley said.

She held her tongue not to add …

Except to say you're a jerk.

Which anyone can see at a glance.

Crites said, "Cathy Lilly knows right well I won't buy the Ogden house for the price she's got in mind. She'll bring it down soon, and she'll bring it down a lot. She don't know no better."

Bill asked, "What do you mean?"

Crites took off his baseball hat and fanned himself with it.

He said, "The damn fool folks in this town are suckers for this 'global warming' crap. They think property values here are down for good. A lot of them are desperate to sell and get the hell out. All I gotta do is wait—they'll sell for peanuts sooner or later. I'm sure you city folks know better. Hell, you're probably in on the whole damn hoax."

Crites was sweating heavily from the heat, and his face was bright red.

He added, "Sure, it's been hot here these last few years. It's been a nasty spell. But it ain't gonna to keep getting worse like those so-called climatologists keep saying, and it won't go on being this hot forever. It's all cyclical-like, you see."

Crites sighed and looked upward, as if basking in dreams of better times to come.

"You mark my words," he said, "we're due for some really fine weather here in Rushville. It'll be here to stay for a good long time. Tourism will come back and property values will go through the roof. And I'll come out on top, and everybody else here'll look like the ignorant crackers they really are."

Crites took a cigar out of his shirt pocket and lit it. Its cheap smell wafted disagreeably in the suffocating air.

He said, "But I don't guess you Feds want to talk to me about real estate. No, I reckon you're here to discuss what happened to Gareth Ogden. Poor bastard, it's a real shame."

Bill asked, "Do you have any ideas about who might have wanted to kill him?"

Crites blew a smoke ring and said, "Hell, it's hard to say. Folks here in Rushville ain't exactly the friendliest people in Mississippi. Lots of 'em would probably like to kill each other if they got the chance, especially in this kind of heat."

Crites shuffled his feet and took another puff on his cigar.

"Sad, though, about Gareth," he added. "Not the nicest fellow in the world—but I guess that's kind of a pot-and-kettle thing for a guy like me to say. But somebody'd have to hate him especially bad to do him in that way—with a hammer, or so they tell me."

Riley asked, "How well did you know him?"

Crites said, "Oh, we were pals, Gareth and me. I used to stop by at nights around his house about the time he was killed for some beer and a chat. I guess I should've been there that night. For sure, I'd have stopped whoever the killer was."

Jenn let out a sarcastic chuckle.

"And how would you have done that?" she asked.

Crites scowled, apparently peeved that she had the nerve to ask him anything at all.

He said, "With my gun, gal. With my gun. I never leave home nights without my Smith & Wesson 627. I carry it in my shoulder holster, where anyone who wants to mess with me can see it. It's perfectly legal, in case you're wondering."

He huffed himself up and added …

"We got proper respect for the Second Amendment here in Mississippi, let me tell you. The law here is open carry, no license required. 'Course, I guess you Feds have got different ideas of what the law should be. Don't start preaching to me about it—that's an argument you're sure to lose."

He let out a grunt of contempt.

"What happened to Gareth is all the proof I need. If you go taking away everybody's guns, folks will use whatever's at hand. A hammer will do as good as anything. So what are you gonna do, start banning hammers? Don't make me laugh."

Riley had heard all this before. Unlike a hammer, a handgun was a tool with only one use, and that was to kill people. But she wasn't interested in opening up what could be a complicated discussion about all that, or about who should wield such tools.

Instead she asked, "Did you try to talk Gareth Ogden into selling his house?"

Crites smiled widely, as if Riley had finally gotten around to asking him something really interesting.

He said, "As a matter of fact, I did. When I'd come over to see him nights, we'd always get around to discussing it sooner or later. And to tell the truth, sometimes we'd get a little het up about it. But he was stubborn about the price, just like his daughter. Said he had to get enough out of it to get well away from here."

With a note of contempt in her voice, Jenn said …

"It sounds like you wanted it really badly. Beachfront property like this has a real future."

Crites looked at the young African-American agent with a sneer.

"I surely did, at that," he said. "And I guess you think that makes me a suspect. Clever girl, aren't you? Takes real intelligence to come to that conclusion. I wouldn't have guessed it from you."

Riley could see that Jenn was quietly seething.

Riley figured she'd better take over asking questions before

Jenn lost her temper.

She said, "Mr. Crites, would you mind telling us where you were when Gareth Ogden was killed"

Crites took a leisurely puff on his cigar and blew the smoke toward Riley and her companions.

He said, "Would you care to remind me exactly when that was?"

Riley stated the date and time of the murder.

Still smiling, Crites said, "Hmm, well. That's kind of hard to say. Maybe I was out playing poker with some of the boys. Maybe I was home watching TV. Or maybe I was drinking whiskey at the bar. Maybe I was with some local hooker—and we've got some nice ones in this town, you'd be surprised."

He grinned and looked at Riley and the others.

"Truth is, you don't know, do you?" he said. "Now the question is—how bad do you suspect me, exactly? Enough to arrest me? Should I be giving my lawyer a ring? If that's the way things are, I guess I could think up a pretty good alibi in a pinch."

Then his sneer turned sinister.

"But things ain't to that point, are they?" he said with a growl. "At least not yet. So I've got no reason to say another word to you Feds. And I'll thank you for hauling your Yankee asses off my property."

He turned back toward his house and started yelling at his workers again.

Jenn took a threatening step toward him, but Riley stopped her.

Riley said to her, "Hey—what do you think you're doing?"

Through clenched teeth, Jenn said, "It's him. He's the killer."

Touching Jenn on the shoulder, Riley said, "Jenn, listen to me. We can't do anything about him now. Let's go talk over what we need to do next."

As Riley and her FBI colleagues and the two local cops walked away from the house, she thought …

Jenn could just be right.

CHAPTER FOURTEEN

Riley could see that Jenn was still angry when the three agents and the two local cops gathered beside their parked cars.

The young agent snapped, "Crites knows we're on to him. He's liable to flee town and disappear if we don't arrest him right now."

Bill said, "We can't arrest him. We don't have anything to bring him in on."

"Hell, he practically confessed!" Jenn retorted.

"He did nothing of the kind," Riley said. "He was definitely taunting us, but we don't know why. It might just be because he doesn't like Feds."

Bill asked Officers Kuehling and Wolfe, "What do the two of you know about Amos Crites? Do you think he's capable of murder?"

Officer Wolfe shrugged and said, "He's always been one mean son-of-a-bitch."

Officer Kuehling added, "Everyone in town knows it. His wife left him years ago because of his abuse. He used to get into fights a lot, especially in bars, and he got arrested for assault a few times. Age has slowed him down. He doesn't fight that much anymore, but he's still mean."

Kuehling paused, then added, "Murder? I don't know about that. But I guess it's hard to say what Amos Crites could be capable of if he got mad enough."

Riley looked back toward the house, where Crites was exchanging banter with his workmen again. He was waving an arm toward Riley and her companions, and his workmen were laughing at whatever he was saying.

Riley thought ...

I guess he thought he pulled a pretty good joke at our expense.

But was Crites really a killer, or ...

Is he just an asshole?

She reminded herself that the two possibilities weren't mutually exclusive.

He might be both an asshole *and* a killer, for all she knew.

But right now, her instincts weren't telling her much of

anything.

Bill said, "Maybe Crites would be more willing to talk to Chief Crane. Maybe we should ask Crane to come by and—"

Kuehling gently interrupted.

"Not a chance. The chief would never make waves with Amos Crites. He owns too much property in town."

Riley nodded as she remembered how angry Crane had been, especially with Riley …

I definitely made an enemy there.

He'd offered them no support at all—just the assistance of these two cops, whom he seemed to hold in low regard.

"I'll give you Feds a chance to see what you can do," he'd said.

"I'll be pretty damned surprised if you find anything."

Riley suppressed a sigh as she thought …

Crane would love to see us fail.

It was apparently up to her, Bill, Jenn, and the two local cops to solve this case on their own, without any help from Crane or anybody else on his force.

Riley thought for a moment, then said to Kuehling and Wolfe …

"Do you know where the paperboy lives? The one who found Ogden's body?"

Kuehling nodded and said, "You can follow us there."

Kuehling and Wolfe got into their police car. When Riley and Bill opened the doors of their FBI vehicle, Jenn just stood sullenly with her arms crossed.

Riley asked, "Jenn, what the hell do you think you're doing?"

"I'm staying here to keep an eye on Crites," Jenn said. "If nobody else is going to do it, it's up to me. I'll follow him around all day if I have to."

Riley said, "He's not a flight risk, Jenn, and you know it. He's got too much property here to make a run for it. And he doesn't think he has anything to fear from us. He'll stay in town."

Although she didn't say so, Riley was also worried that Jenn might wind up in a physical altercation with the guy. Riley was sure Crites would be delighted to bring a charge of harassment against them. That was the last thing they all needed right now.

When Jenn continued to balk at getting into the car, Bill barked impatiently …

"Roston, let's go. That's a goddamn order."

With a low growl of complaint, Jenn gave in and climbed into the back seat. Riley and Bill also got in, and Bill started up the car to follow the cops' car.

Jenn muttered to Riley, "I suppose this is where you accuse me of not being objective."

Riley felt her own anger rising now.

She knew perfectly well that Jenn was reacting to Crites's unconcealed racism. Riley had felt a similar fury at misogynistic jerks who didn't think women should be FBI agents. And Jenn had to deal with both of those problems. But an agent had to keep those personal resentments under control.

And now Jenn was not only unloading her frustrations on her partners, she was getting dangerously close to accusing Riley herself of harboring racist feelings.

Riley and Jenn hadn't been working together for very long, and although they've had some conflicts early on, nothing like this had ever come up between them before.

Riley fought down a rash urge to call Jenn out about her hinted assumption, to have it out with her and clear the air, but ...

Don't do it, she thought.

For one thing, a guy like Crites would be thrilled to know he was having a toxic effect on their relationship.

Instead she said ...

"Jenn, stop thinking like that. We'll get to the bottom of this. And if Crites is our man, we'll bring him in."

They all fell silent as Bill continued to drive them through the little town.

Riley found herself remembering what Crites had said a few minutes ago about the people here in Rushville ...

"Lots of 'em would probably like to kill each other if they got the chance, especially in this kind of heat."

Whatever else Crites may have been lying about, he could be telling the truth about that. Rushville seemed to bring out something mean in people, and she didn't think it was just because of the weather.

It occurred to Riley that she, Bill, and Jenn had to be careful. This oppressive, suffocating, and disagreeable atmosphere could get to them too.

We might turn mean ourselves before we know it.

CHAPTER FIFTEEN

During the short drive to the house where the paperboy lived, Riley was feeling apprehensive. She always dreaded talking to traumatized witnesses, especially children.

They followed a narrow street into a neighborhood quite a few blocks away from the beach. The area was desolate and rundown—no sidewalks, patchy grass in the sandy soil, and rows of beat-up ranch houses badly in need of paint.

When Riley and her colleagues got out of their car, she was startled by a cloud of insects that buzzed around them.

Mosquitos, she realized.

As Riley started swatting at the swarm, the two local cops came trotting up.

Officer Kuehling was holding out a small plastic spray bottle. "You'll need some repellent," she said,

Wolfe added, "Mosquitos will eat you alive, late in the day like this and away from the water."

As the young woman began spraying Riley and her colleagues where their skin was exposed, she said, "Don't worry, this stuff is made of natural ingredients—mostly lemon eucalyptus oil. We've been using it for years and it does the trick. We'll buy you some as soon as we get a chance."

Kuehling sprayed the agents' hands and told them to rub the oil on their faces, applying it only lightly on the ears and avoiding the mouth and eyes altogether.

Wolfe said, "This has been an especially nasty summer for mosquitos. We've had four or five cases of the West Nile virus so far this year, right here in Rushville."

Riley and her colleagues exchanged uneasy glances. She knew they were all thinking the same thing.

They were used to risking their lives and dangerous circumstances. But the possibility of catching a potentially serious mosquito-borne disease was nothing to scoff at.

Riley had read awful things about the West Nile virus. Although most infected people never showed symptoms, those who did suffered from ailments ranging from headaches, nausea, and vomiting to paralysis, coma, and possibly even death.

Another reason to get this case finished up as fast as we can, Riley thought.

Jenn finished with the spray bottle, and the group walked toward the house. They saw someone standing just inside the screen door—a lean, dark-haired man with a tired, sad expression.

From behind the screen the man said, "FBI, I take it."

Riley was relieved that he didn't sound unwelcoming. All three agents took out their badges and introduced themselves.

The man nodded and opened the screen door.

He said, "Come on in, get away from the bugs. I've sprayed all the screens, so that keeps most of them out. I wish I could do something about the heat, but …"

Riley and her companions walked into the house, which was stiflingly hot even though a big fan was running in the living room.

No air conditioning, Riley realized.

There hadn't been any air conditioning back at the Ogden house either, but the air had been fresher back there close to the water. Here, the heat was considerably more oppressive.

She glanced around the small living room. The furniture was worn and old, and it looked like it had been bought cheap to begin with. Although it looked like the inhabitants did their best to keep the place clean and neat, odors of mold and mildew hung in the air.

The man nodded to the two local cops and invited all five of them to sit down.

Then he sat down himself and said, "I heard you FBI folks got here today. Word gets around fast in a town like this. I figured you'd come around here soon. I'm Wyatt's older brother, Brandon. It's just him and me who live here anymore."

Riley asked, "Is Wyatt here? If so, we'd like to talk with him."

Brandon sighed and said, "The truth is, I wish you would. He's been having a rough time ever since … well, you know. He has some OK days, but other days he shuts himself up in his room and barely talks to me."

Riley could see a world of sadness and concern in Brandon's eyes. His face was heavily lined, and his hair was sprinkled slightly with gray. When she'd first seen him, Riley had thought he was well into his thirties. But now she realized he was probably much younger—in his mid-twenties, maybe.

He's lived a hard life, she thought.

Jenn asked him, "Have you tried getting your brother into

counseling?"

Brandon said, "Yeah, I took him to the local pediatric clinic a couple of times. The therapist there is no good, though. And anyway, I can't afford it, even on the clinic's sliding scale."

He appeared to be genuinely pained to admit to his poverty.

Riley asked, "Could you describe your living situation?"

Brandon squinted a little. Riley sensed that he was reluctant to dig into some bitter memories.

"Mom died in the big hurricane a few years back. Anyhow, she'd been pretty much a basket case for years—ever since Dad left us, back when I was about Wyatt's age. It's been up to me to pay the rent and keep food on the table all this time."

Brandon shuffled his feet and continued, "I manage to keep us going, taking whatever jobs I can get—garbage collecting, handy work, bagging groceries. Once in a while I get lucky with some construction work, but that's pretty rare in a dying town like this."

He fell silent for a moment, then said, "My first job was a paper route. I figured it would be a safe job for Wyatt to start out with."

He shrugged and added, "But what the hell do I know? I didn't even know that Old Man Ogden was on Wyatt's route. Not that my knowing would have made any difference, I don't suppose …"

His voice faded again. Then he looked at visitors and said …

"But I'm being rude. You folks must be parched. I've got some iced tea in the fridge. Would you like some?"

Riley and her four companions said yes.

As Brandon got out of his chair to head to the kitchen, Riley asked him, "Is it OK if I have a word with your brother now?"

Brandon nodded and led Riley down a hallway. Riley noticed that a doorway on one side of the hall was boarded up. Brandon knocked on the door on the opposite side.

"Hey, Wyatt," he called out gently. "Someone's hear to talk to you. Can we come in?"

After a pause, a young voice said …

"Sure."

Brandon opened the door, and he and Riley walked into the boy's bedroom.

Wyatt was sitting on the edge of his bed looking out the room's only window into the back yard. Riley considered the room remarkably neat for that of a teenager—certainly neater than how her own daughters kept their rooms. But Riley quickly realized that there was a reason for the lack of clutter …

Hardly any toys. No kid-type junk.

It was obvious that Brandon Hitt hadn't been able to afford to buy much for his little brother over the years. And there had been no one else to fill that gap. Riley thought Christmas mornings must have been pretty much a non-event in this household, at least as far as Wyatt was concerned.

Except for his light blond hair, the boy looked a lot like a shorter version of Brandon—thin and wiry and awkward-looking.

Brandon said in a gentle voice …

"Wyatt, this is Agent Paige, and she's with the FBI. She'd like to talk with you a little."

Still staring out the window, Wyatt nodded indifferently.

Brandon exchanged glances with Riley and left the room, closing the door behind him. Riley was relieved not to have to tell him she'd prefer talking to the boy alone.

She sat down on the bed beside Wyatt and said nothing.

Let him talk first, she thought.

After a few seconds, Wyatt said in a hoarse, breaking voice, "I guess you want to ask me a lot of questions. Like the cops did."

Riley paused for a moment, then said, "Just tell me what happened that morning as well as you can."

In a rather mechanical voice, Wyatt related how he'd been on his early morning paper route delivering a newspaper to Gareth Ogden's house. Ogden had been a stickler for how he wanted his paper delivered, so Wyatt had walked up onto the porch to put the paper behind the screen door …

"And that's when I saw him," Wyatt said.

He shuddered deeply, then added, "I'm not sure what happened right after that. They say I called the cops. I was sitting on the steps when the cops got there. I don't remember much else. They say I was in shock."

Riley quickly realized …

He just told me everything he possibly can.

There was no point in pushing for any half-forgotten details that would probably prove unhelpful to her anyway.

Riley said, "I'm going to tell you a secret. I'm not really here to ask you a lot of questions. I know you've answered a lot of those already. I just want to check and see how you're doing. How are you holding up?"

Wyatt shuddered silently.

Then, as if in answer to Riley's question, he pointed out into the back yard, which was small and barren.

He said, "See that place where the ground is kind of hollow? A big tree used to be there. It got blown down in the hurricane. It fell on the house."

Riley thought hard, trying to process exactly what Wyatt was getting at.

Then she remembered the boarded up doorway in the hallway.

Another room must have once been there. A bedroom.

In a low voice, almost a whisper, Riley said …

"That's how your mom died, isn't it?"

The boy nodded and wiped away a single tear.

Then he said, "Mom was in bed when the tree fell. I was in here. I was sleeping. I was … safe. When I heard what happened, I ran across the hall and …"

Riley realized with a shiver …

He found his own mother's dead body.

She had a brief flash of the memory that always haunted her …

She was just a little girl in a candy store …a man with a gun shot Mommy in the chest…

Riley had seen her own mother killed and had suffered years of pain and guilt even though she could not have prevented what happened.

She understood very well how finding Gareth Ogden's body had reawakened that earlier trauma for Wyatt Hitt. Now the boy was struggling with a tangle of chaotic emotions, especially guilt and fear.

Trying to keep his voice under control he said …

"Mom always said I was the reason Dad left. She said he couldn't put up with me, and it was a long time ago, but I remember Dad yelling at me a lot. Mom said I still wasn't any use to her or anybody else. I wonder if maybe she was right. And if maybe she'd been here in my room and I'd been over there …"

Riley swallowed hard.

She said, "Wyatt, you mustn't think like that."

"I can't help it," Wyatt said, his voice squawking a little with emotion. "It's been bothering me for a long time. And now there's something else …"

Seeming to gather up his nerve, he continued …

"Old Mr. Ogden—he was mean and I didn't like him."

Riley wrinkled her brow, trying to understand what Wyatt

meant.

"Why does that matter?" she asked him.

Spitting the words out anxiously, Wyatt said, "I didn't like him because he was always yelling at me, saying I couldn't do anything right, just like Dad used to do. I didn't like him and now he's dead. I still don't like him. I feel like that's wrong. I feel like maybe I should like him now. But I can't."

Riley's heart ached for him.

She said, "Wyatt, nothing you're talking about was your fault. It wasn't your fault your dad left, or your mom died, or Mr. Ogden got killed."

Wyatt wiped away another tear.

"Yeah, that was what that therapist guy told me," he said. "But he was really stupid."

Riley chuckled slightly and patted him on the shoulder.

She said, "I hope you think I'm smarter."

Wyatt laughed just a little as well.

"Yeah, you're lots smarter than him," he said.

Riley said, "Well, here's one way to think about Mr. Ogden. I've talked to several people since I've been in town. As far as I can tell, hardly anyone liked him. Is that true?"

Wyatt nodded.

Riley added, "Do you think everybody else is feeling guilty for not liking him?"

Wyatt shook his head.

Riley said, "Well, there you have it. You shouldn't feel guilty either. About anything."

Wyatt let out a sound that seemed like both a sob and a relieved chuckle.

He said, "Thanks for … you know … talking to me about all this."

Riley said, "Do you ever talk to your brother about these feelings?"

"No," Wyatt said. "I don't want to bother him about it. I'm enough trouble for him already."

Riley almost gasped with pity.

"He doesn't think you're any trouble," Riley said. "He loves you. He'd do anything for you. I know that. And you need to talk to him about everything you just told me. He'll understand, and he'll help. Promise me you'll do that."

"I promise," Wyatt said.

Riley got up and left the room. She went back to the living room where she found Brandon talking quietly with Bill, Jenn, and the two local cops.

Riley said to Brandon, "We're going to leave now. You should talk to your brother right away. I think it will help now."

Brandon looked surprised but pleased.

Riley and her companions left the house. On the way to their cars, Riley said to Officers Kuehling and Wolfe ...

"My colleagues and I need to find a motel. Can you show us a good place to stay the night?"

Kuehling laughed a little and said, "Well, maybe not a *good* place. But yeah, we can find you something."

Kuehling and Wolfe headed for their car, and Riley and her two colleagues got into theirs. As Bill pulled away to follow the two local cops, Jenn asked Riley ...

"What happened back there? Was the kid able to tell you anything?"

Suddenly Riley realized she was on the verge of tears.

But the last thing she wanted to do right now was talk about what had just happened.

It was late in the day, and she was tired, and it was getting dark outside.

But she couldn't help wondering ...

Why does it always *seem so dark in this town?*

CHAPTER SIXTEEN

Jenn shivered as she pushed open the glass door and walked into the diner.

Too much air conditioning, she realized.

The cold was shocking in contrast to the heat outside, which hadn't let up much even now that it was evening.

"This is an improvement," Bill commented, following close behind her.

Riley gazed around the tarnished chrome décor and said, "Well, it's convenient."

The two young local cops, Kuehling and Wolfe, had led them to the motel next door and had pointed out the diner. The cops had been apologetic before they went on their way. They'd said there weren't any better places to spend the night in Rushville, especially not in August when a lot of things that weren't already closed shut down for the hottest summer month.

The motel had plenty of rooms open and they each had a bedroom and bath that connected with a living room. "The suite," the desk clerk had called it. But those rooms smelled as stale and moldy as the house where Brandon and Wyatt Hitt lived.

Jenn fought down a groan of irritation. She didn't like this town at all.

A cheerful hostess in a checkered dress greeted them with menus. As the woman led them through the dining area, Jenn saw that the place was crowded—and unfriendly, or so it seemed to her. Almost everyone looked up from their meals to stare at the agents as the hostess escorted them to a booth.

Jenn felt a different kind of chill now.

All these white faces, she thought.

It felt odd that it should bother her. After all, she often found herself the only African-American in many situations, and she seldom gave it any thought. On most cases she was more likely to run into overt sexism than racism.

But she was in the Deep South now, and things felt very different.

She told herself not to get paranoid.

After all, few of the people here seemed to be staring at her in particular. They seemed to be more interested in the whole group.

She remembered that Brandon Hitt had said …

"Word gets around fast in a town like this."

Everybody apparently knew that they were FBI agents. And of course everybody would know about the murders they were investigating. Back at Quantico, Bill had said this town wasn't used to violent crime, so their presence was bound to be a major topic of conversation.

She and her colleagues sat down in the booth and perused their menus. Fried chicken was the specialty of the place, of course, so that was what they all ordered when a server came to their booth.

Jenn was aware that her colleagues were avoiding talking about any specifics of the case. She knew that none of them had anything new to say about it, but she thought they should make some decisions about what they were going to do tomorrow. Instead, Riley mentioned that she needed to call home tonight and check in with her kids. Bill was trying to figure out just what he could report to Meredith.

As the food arrived and their conversation continued, Jenn was struck by how Amos Crites's name was scarcely mentioned, except as someone they needed to keep track of.

Had Riley and Bill already decided that Crites wasn't the killer?

Jenn remembered what Jeffreys had told her when she'd said they should arrest Crites …

"We don't have anything to bring him in on."

It was true, of course.

Jenn now realized that she'd overreacted to Amos Crites's palpable bigotry, especially his condescension when he'd said …

"Clever girl, aren't you?"

Her anger swelled again as she remembered how he'd "congratulated" her on her intelligence for considering him a suspect …

"I wouldn't have guessed it from you."

Now Jenn felt embarrassed that she'd let him push her buttons like that. Besides, she knew better than to think the man's bigotry had anything to do with whether or not he was a murderer.

She felt especially bad about her sharp words to Riley in the car …

"I suppose this is where you accuse me of not being objective."

80

A cheap shot, she admitted.

She'd only known Riley for a few months now, but she knew perfectly well that she was no bigot. She would apologize when she found the right moment to bring that up again.

The waitress brought their orders, and Jenn was grateful to have something else to focus on for a while. The fried chicken was surprisingly good, so the conversation came to a halt while they all enjoyed their food.

When she had finished as much of the meal as she could, Jenn excused herself to go to the restroom. The women's room was down a short hallway and around a corner from the men's room, where the hall formed a cul-de-sac that ended with a fire exit. While she was in there, she paused to look at herself in the mirror and felt a sudden surge of pride.

An experienced FBI agent!

No one else was in the restroom, so she took her badge out of her purse and looked at it.

She was proud of that. Sometimes it really amazed her that she had accomplished so much in such a short time. Not long ago, she'd never have imagined that she'd pursue a career in law enforcement. Instead, she'd seemed fated for a life of crime.

Jenn shuddered as she remembered. Her teenage years had been spent in a foster home in Aunt Cora's care. The wily woman had been training her kids to become part of her own criminal network. She'd succeeded with all of her young charges ... except for Jenn.

Seized by a spasm of unworthiness, Jenn folded up her badge and put it back in her purse.

After all, Aunt Cora remained a presence in her life—still willing to help Jenn in her new career in exchange for questionable favors.

Thinking about all this, Jenn felt a resurgence of gratitude toward Riley.

Riley was the only person who knew the truth, both about Jenn's past and her continuing relationship with Aunt Cora.

More than that, Riley understood and sympathized. After all, she had had her own entanglement with a criminal mastermind, the brilliant escaped convict Shane Hatcher. Hatcher had been Riley's frequent ally—but at a terrible moral cost.

That was all over with now, of course. Hatcher was back in prison where he belonged.

Jenn knew more than anybody else about Riley's secret, just as Riley knew all about hers.

Jenn smiled at her reflection as she thought about the bond that had grown between them. Jenn and Riley were a lot alike in many ways, including a mutual willingness to bend and even break the rules.

Looking at herself in the mirror, Jenn muttered aloud …

"Riley's my best friend."

She reminded herself again that she owed Riley an apology.

As she walked out of the restroom into the dimly lit hallway, she noticed two large shadows cast from the dining room light.

As she took another step, she saw that two big men were standing just around the corner.

Jenn felt a rush of alarm. Were they waiting for her to come out of the restroom?

This looks like trouble, she thought.

CHAPTER SEVENTEEN

Jenn backed up a little and stood stone still outside the restroom door, watching the shadows that were cast from around the corner. Two men were standing in the narrow hallway and she could hear them speaking to one another in lowered voices.

Both her experience and instincts told her that they were waiting for her—and that they meant trouble.

She figured they must be pretty stupid, picking a fight in a public place like this …

Or maybe …

Maybe they were sure that others would happily join them.

Jenn would have preferred to settle this quietly, with no fighting at all. She thought maybe she could escape through the door right behind her at the end of the hallway. But when she looked, she saw that the door bore a familiar warning sign …

FIRE DOOR
ALARM WILL SOUND IF DOOR IS OPENED

Did she want to sound an alarm?

Was it a good idea to get the whole diner up in arms? Of course she could count on Riley and Bill to come to her aid. But what kind of chaos might follow?

Jenn spent a second too long trying to decide.

The nearest man had turned and looked around the corner. Before she could make another move, he was upon her.

He grabbed her and thrust her violently backward against the restroom door. The door swung open, and Jenn staggered back inside the restroom.

In an instant, both of the burly men pushed through the door and stood facing her.

As the light fell on their faces, she recognized them.

They were two of the men who had been working on the roof of Amos Crites's house. But they looked a lot bigger and stronger than they had from the ground.

One of the men smiled an evil smile and said …

"Why looky here, Russ. Doesn't this girl look familiar?"

The other man smiled and said, "I believe she does, Lee. I think she's one of them Feds who bothered our buddy Amos awhile back."

The one named Lee squinted and frowned at her and said ...

"I do believe my brother here is right. And as I remember, you were *especially* rude to our buddy Amos, more than your two friends. I think you hurt Amos's feelings. Don't you think so, Russ?"

"She surely did hurt his feelings," the one named Russ said. "Amos told me so himself."

His brother said to Jenn, "Is that any way to behave, a stranger who's just arrived in town, depending on our kind hospitality?"

Jenn's mind clicked away as she assessed her physical situation, especially the size of the restroom and the space between herself and her adversaries.

As the one named Lee stepped toward her, she said ...

"Aren't you afraid I'll yell for help?"

Lee chuckled and said, "What kind of help do you think you'll get? We folks look out for each other. Besides, you seem like the quiet type. I don't take you for much of a screamer."

At that moment he reached out for her.

As she grabbed him by the wrist, Jenn muttered, "You're right about that."

While he was still in forward motion, she twisted his arm over his head, forcing him to bend sharply and stumble forward. His nose smashed violently against the restroom sink.

As Lee tumbled to the floor in a daze, Jenn turned toward Russ, who looked momentarily startled. She was pleased to see that she had exactly the space she needed to land one crucial blow.

She reared back, then kicked as high as she could, connecting perfectly with Russ's chin. Russ flew backward so hard that the restroom door broke into splinters.

There he lay, stretched through the hole in the door, with his legs in the restroom and the rest of his body out in the hallway.

Before Jenn could pause to savor her handiwork, she heard loud voices and a clatter of many footsteps.

Oh my God, she thought.

All the men in the place are after me now.

As the voices and footsteps approached in the hallway, Jenn was surprised to hear general laughter.

A group of men stood looking down at Russ's prostrate body, grinning and chuckling with delight.

"Well, whaddya know," one man said, peering inside the restroom, where Jenn was standing beside her other semi-conscious would-be attacker. "It looks like the mighty King brothers got both their butts whipped by a girl!"

A couple of the men stooped down and dragged Russ to his feet. Two other men came into the restroom and did the same with the one who was crumpled on his knees, his nose bleeding profusely. Lee seemed to have no idea where he was or what was going on.

She heard a man in the hall say, "Somebody call the cops to come and pick these boys up."

Another man gave Jenn a friendly pat on the arm.

"Congratulations, little lady. You gave the King brothers a lesson they've had coming for a long time."

The man led Jenn into the hallway, where she was greeted by whistles and cheers and slaps on the back. The man escorted her back into the dining room, where the hostess in the checkered dress stood smiling.

The woman said to Jenn, "Nice going, honey. How'd you and your friends like some dessert on the house? Our apple pie's good and fresh, and we've got vanilla ice cream."

Feeling more than a little dazed herself now, Jenn said …

"Um … that would be nice."

Riley and Agent Jeffreys were standing near their booth, with their mouths hanging open.

Riley said, "Jenn, what the hell just happened?"

Jenn laughed nervously and said …

"I guess I just took down a couple of town bullies. Let's go sit down, I'll tell you all about it over dessert."

*

After they heard all the details of the attack on Jenn and finished their pie, Riley and her colleagues headed back to their motel. Riley was glad to get back to her own room. It had been a long day, and she was tired and more than ready to go to sleep.

The air conditioner was making sputtering sounds, and it started rumbling like a freight train when she turned it up higher.

Riley sighed.

Which was going to be worse—listening to this air conditioner all night, or suffering through the heat without it?

I'm probably not going to get a lot of sleep either way, she figured.

Riley decided to let the machine run at least for a while. She sat down on the edge of her bed and thought about what had just happened back at the diner.

She smiled as she thought about how Jenn had dealt with her two attackers. Her smile widened as she remembered the general enthusiasm that had ensued …

Pretty good dessert, too.

Even so, Riley had noticed that not everyone in the crowded diner had been pleased. A few customers had left the place in a silent huff. At least some of the others had glowered at Jenn until they all left the place.

A black woman in law enforcement, Riley thought.

It had pushed some angry buttons among at least some of those people—although those buttons could have been related to black, female, law, or any combination of the three.

It had been a scene that people would be talking about. Now there was a worrisome possibility that there would be further repercussions.

She was also troubled by the fact that Jenn's attackers had been friends of Amos Crites, and they'd seemed to be acting on his behalf.

She wondered again whether Crites was guilty of murder. After all, he did have a motive for killing Ogden. He wanted Ogden's property.

Riley made a mental note to find out if any property issue might have been involved in the murder of the Bonnett family ten years back.

If Crites was a killer, were Lee and Russ King his accomplices in some way?

Had they been trying to intimidate the agents into abandoning their investigation?

Fat chance of that, Riley thought. *But they probably weren't bright enough to realize that threats didn't work on FBI agents.*

The two thugs were in jail right now, and she wished she could go there and ask them some serious questions. But of course she knew that Chief Crane would never allow her to do anything like that. The status of Riley and her colleagues here in Rushville was nebulous at best.

Were they officially on the case, or weren't they?

Chief Crane would almost certainly say they weren't, and that didn't bode well for their investigation. Riley knew that Bill was in his own room right now calling Brent Meredith to update him about their activities that day. While Meredith might well agree that that a potential serial killer was at large here, even he couldn't legitimize their investigation all by himself.

Riley sighed aloud. She could only hope they could stay here long enough to do their work.

Maybe another day will be enough, she thought.

Meanwhile, she looked at her watch and saw how late it was getting. And of course, it was two hours later back in Fredericksburg. She needed to check in at home before the kids went to sleep.

She called on her cell phone, and April answered.

"Hey, Mom. How's the case going?"

"It's hard to say," Riley said, not wanting to get into all that. "How are things at home? How's school?"

"OK, I guess," April said. "But …"

April's voice faded, and Riley felt a tingle of apprehension.

Then April said, "Mom, I'm worried about Jilly. She's been all sad since you left. I even caught her crying in her bedroom this afternoon."

Her worry rising, Riley asked, "Did she say what was wrong?"

"No, and she got kind of huffy about it when I asked. She said she wasn't crying at all, it was just the sniffles. But I know what I heard and saw. And she won't spend any time with me."

April paused again, then said, "Mom, how soon do you think you could get home? I don't want to alarm you or anything but … I think maybe we need you here. Or Jilly does, anyway."

Riley didn't like what she was hearing.

"Could you get Jilly on the phone?" Riley said.

"I'll try," April said.

She heard April's footsteps as she made her way from her own bedroom to Jilly's. Then she heard a knock at the door and April calling out …

"Mom wants to talk to you."

Then came the sound of a door opening and Jilly's voice on the phone.

"Hi, Mom. Catch any bad guys yet?"

Riley was surprised that Jilly sounded quite cheerful.

"Not yet," Riley said.

"Well, keep at it. I know you will. And kick some butt when you get a chance."

Riley chuckled nervously.

"I'll try to do that," she said. "Actually, my partner kind of beat me to it."

"Really?" Jilly said. "Tell me about it!"

"I will when I get home," Riley said.

She wished she could see Jilly's face. It was hard to tell just from her voice exactly what was going on with her.

Cautiously, Riley said, "Jilly—do you want me to come home?"

"Huh?" Jilly said.

Riley sputtered, "I—I mean, are you doing OK? Would it help if I was there?"

A chilly silence fell.

Then Jilly said, "What did April tell you?"

Riley gulped hard and said, "Well, April said … she's kind of worried that maybe …"

There was a sharpness in Jilly's voice now.

"Well, April's being all weird about things. I don't know what she's thinking. And whatever she told you about me, it's not true, OK? I'm fine."

"OK," Riley said. "I'm glad to hear it."

What else can I say? Riley thought.

Sounding markedly less cheerful now, Jilly said …

"Look, I've got to get back to my homework. And you've got your own work to do. So catch some bad guys, OK? Do it for me. I'm counting on it."

"I'll do that," Riley said.

"I mean it," Jilly said. "The last thing in the world I want is for you to worry about me."

"OK," Riley said.

They said "I love you" to each other and ended the call.

Riley sat on the bed staring at the cell phone.

Something's not right, she thought.

Jilly's tone of voice just now reminded Riley of their vacation, when she'd asked Jilly how she'd gotten that small cut on her thigh …

And she got another cut on her forearm before that.

Riley felt tempted to order tickets and fly right back home.

After all, if she and her partners *weren't* officially on the case, how badly was she really needed here?

Surely Bill and Jenn could handle things in her absence.

But then she remembered what Jilly had said …

"The last thing in the world I want is for you to worry about me."

And also …

"Catch some bad guys, OK? Do it for me. I'm counting on it."

Jilly sounded like she really meant it—for what reason, Riley didn't know.

I'd better take her at her word, Riley decided.

Riley got up and walked to the room's front window. She opened the curtain and looked out into the sleepy street. Rushville looked so peaceful right now.

But again, Riley sensed the presence of someone lurking outside.

He's out there, she thought. *Ogden's killer is out there. The Bonnett family's killer hasn't left town.*

She got a strong but momentary sense of a lurking man with a hammer in his hand—not physically here outside her window, but somewhere in this quiet little town.

He wasn't very far away, and he was definitely going to strike again.

CHAPTER EIGHTEEN

The man stood staring at the little house on the opposite side of the street.

It was night, and the drapes in the front window were wide open. Although he himself was safely concealed by shadow, he could see the whole family in the well-lighted living room.

The man was sitting in his overstuffed chair staring blankly at the TV.

The two kids—a boy and a younger girl—were arguing and chasing each other around.

But it was the woman—the wife and mother—who held the man's interest.

She was standing in an archway looking at her family. He couldn't make out her facial expression from this distance, but her body language was plenty eloquent. Her arms were crossed and she was slouched over in an attitude of abject despair.

Life had disappointed her, he could clearly see that, and now here she was living with shattered hopes and dreams. It must be a hard life for a housewife cooped up in such a small home with a family that made her miserable.

And of course, he knew who she was …

Vanessa Pinker.

He didn't know her well, but he knew her name. And she knew his name too. They'd even spoken to each other earlier today. In a town like this, people mostly knew each other's names, even if they didn't know much about each other.

He smiled a little at the thought …

Nobody here knows me.

Not even the people who think *they know me.*

He murmured aloud …

"Come on out, Vanessa. Don't make me wait. I'm tired of waiting. And you're tired, too. You're tired of life."

He chuckled grimly and added softly …

"I can help with that. Just give me a chance."

He'd been following her around for more than a week now—ever since he'd killed that Ogden fellow in his house down by the beach.

He'd been patient—and he'd been proud of his patience.

But now his patience was wearing thin.

Indeed, his whole body suddenly twitched with irritation. The heat certainly didn't help. Even the dark wasn't cool these days. Standing next to a scrubby tree, he could feel no breeze. And all was quiet except for the steady rumble of crickets and a single car engine a few blocks away.

He wondered—how was the heat inside the house? He could see that the family had a fan going. Was their air conditioning working? People all over town were complaining these days that theirs had broken down.

The windows to the house were closed, so apparently the family's air conditioning must not have kicked out completely. But the heat out here was certainly wearing him down.

He knew that, logically, he could just choose someone else.

He laughed a little at the very idea ...

Logic's got nothing to do with this.

He had no logical reason for killing anyone, and certainly none for choosing Vanessa for his next victim. His actions grew from some internal urge that he had to respect, something that told him exactly what needed to be done—and the kind of man he needed to *be,* not just for himself, but for everybody.

He'd known without knowing why that he'd had to kill Ogden.

And now he knew the same thing about Vanessa Pinker.

The idea of killing women was appealing to him more and more, but that was hardly the point.

The only thing that mattered was the deed itself—its integrity, its swiftness, its quiet brutality.

Of course it was important for him to keep in mind ...

The FBI is in town.

Everybody in Rushville knew that by now. That hardly worried him. In fact, it heightened his excitement. He was delighted at the thought of the Feds spinning their wheels, looking for a motive for Ogden's murder, perhaps even thinking they'd found one.

But any theories they managed to devise would be dashed by the next murder.

What motive could anyone have for killing an ordinary small-town housewife?

Certainly no one would ever suspect *him.*

The most important thing was not to get ahead of himself, not to do anything rash or impetuous or ill-timed, to wait for and seize the precise and perfect moment.

Discipline, he reminded himself.

Discipline was so very, very important.

Discipline was what had been lacking ten years ago.

The Bonnett family had died much too sloppily.

He was pleased at the swift, clean blow that had killed Gareth Ogden—a single blow to the forehead. He had to achieve the same success with Vanessa. Nothing less than perfection would suffice.

As he stood watching, the woman turned and wearily walked away out of sight.

Nothing more to see, he thought.

As he stepped out of the shadows and started to walk home, he remembered overhearing some kids scaring each other by talking about Ogden's murder. They'd also been also talking about the family that had been slain before they could remember, before some of them had even been born.

And now they even had a nickname for the killer …

The Carpenter.

"The Carpenter is back again," the kids kept saying.

He smiled.

It was an apt moniker for a killer with a hammer.

It was also suggestive of dexterity and skill.

As he walked through the streets lined with quiet houses, he thought about the terror he was only beginning to unleash.

It'll do Rushville good, he thought.

A few murders were just what this town needed to bring it to life again.

CHAPTER NINETEEN

When Riley walked into the diner early the next morning she was wondering what kind of attitude they'd run into today. Bill and Jenn were following close behind her, and she thought they must be a bit apprehensive too.

A different hostess met them with menus.

"Why, you must be the FBI folks," she said rather sternly. Then with a wink she added, "Now you're not going to go busting up the place again this morning, are you? A couple of workmen are putting in a new door to the women's room right now. The owner'd be happier not to have to do any more repairs."

Riley and her colleagues chuckled. Sure enough, Riley could hear the sound of power tools from the direction of the restrooms.

Riley looked around the place, which was crowded for breakfast. This time the glances they got looked friendly enough—but curious, too. Riley guessed that everybody here knew what had happened last night.

Riley said to the hostess, "Don't worry, we'll try our best to behave."

Jenn added, "As long as nobody else tries to pick a fight."

The hostess called out to everybody in the diner …

"Y'hear that, folks? The FBI wants to keep things peaceable this morning. Is everybody OK with that?"

Riley was startled to hear general laughter and yelps of approval.

The hostess said, "Come on in, a couple of local cops are already waiting for you."

As the hostess led them to a large booth, Riley was pleased to see that Officers Kuehling and Wolfe were sitting there drinking coffee. Yesterday evening the two cops had said they'd meet Riley and her colleagues here if they could.

As Riley, Bill, and Jenn sat down with them, Kuehling said, "Chief Crane said it would be OK for us to help you out today."

Riley said, "I'm glad to hear that."

Wolfe laughed and added, "It's not out of the goodness of his heart, believe me. He'd still rather you just picked up and left, and he wanted us to tell you that. He's letting us work with you because, well ..."

Kuehling finished his thought ...

"He says we're not much good to him. He can spare us easily."

Riley smiled. She'd guessed as much yesterday. As far as she was concerned, it was another sign that Chief Crane wasn't very bright. Riley was still impressed by the ability Kuehling had shown yesterday to describe how Ogden's empty living room had looked at the time of the murder.

Riley said, "I think Chief Crane underestimates your ability, Officer Kuehling."

Kuehling blushed and ducked her head.

She said shyly, "Um, Agent Paige—I'm feeling pretty daunted by having you folks around. I mean that in a good way, I think you're just awesome. But I'd feel more at ease if you just called me Sam—short for Samantha. It's what everybody calls me."

Then with a nod toward her partner she added with playful grin ...

"And you can call *him* Dominic."

Dominic laughed and said to Riley and her colleagues, "That's Sam for you. Always calling the shots for us both. Which is OK, because she does most of the thinking. Anyway, I'm fine with Dominic."

Riley eyed the two young cops with interest. It was obvious that Sam had the talent and brains of the team. But Dominic didn't seem to resent that. They seemed to be good friends and good partners.

The five of them ordered breakfast and began to talk about the case. They all had to admit that they seemed to be at a dead end. It would soon be two weeks since Gareth Ogden had been murdered. There had been no sign of the killer since then.

Then Dominic said, "Or maybe he's killed somebody else that we don't know about."

Sam looked at her partner and said, "Do you mean like he hid the body?"

Dominic shrugged and said, "I dunno. Something like that."

Riley said, "It's an interesting idea, but I doubt it."

Bill explained, "Statistically, most serial killers are consistent about how they deal with the body—whether they move it, hide it, or leave it right where the murder happened. Some always conceal it and others always want it to be found."

Jenn added, "Consistency is part of our problem. Was Ogden killed by the same person who murdered the Bonnett family? Aside from the murder weapon, there aren't a lot of similarities."

Riley sensed that Jenn's brain was clicking away. She waited to hear what she might say next.

Finally Jenn said, "Riley, I think I owe you an apology."

"For what?" Riley said.

"I got awfully sharp and defensive yesterday about Amos Crites. I kind of implied that you thought I was ... well, you know."

Riley understood what she meant. She was referring to her remark in the car yesterday ...

"I suppose this is where you accuse me of not being objective."

Riley was relieved that they could put that hurtful moment behind them.

She smiled at Jenn and said, "It's OK, Jenn. You were frustrated, and with good reason."

Poking at her scrambled eggs with her fork, Jenn said, "Still, I can't help thinking Crites did it. Killed Ogden, I mean."

Bill said, "Explain your theory."

Jenn shrugged and said, "Well, it's not like I've got any amazing insights. It's pretty obvious that Crites had a motive. He wanted to buy Ogden's house. And now that Ogden's dead, he's liable to buy it more cheaply, sooner or later."

Jenn paused, then added, "But I don't think he had anything to do with what happened to the Bonnetts. I think he used a similar MO just to throw us off his trail, just to confuse us."

Sam shook her head. "I'm sorry, but ... I don't agree. I still think the same person killed the Bonnetts *and* Gareth Ogden. That doesn't eliminate Crites as a suspect, though. He might have killed the Bonnetts back then and Ogden a couple of weeks ago."

Riley mulled it over ...

If Crites is trying to confuse us, his tactic is working.

And yet ...

"We're still in the same situation as yesterday," Riley said. "Chief Crane isn't going to help us investigate Crites. Keeping watch on him would mean rotating watchers, but that's not going to happen. If he's our killer, we've got to catch him some other way."

She took a sip of coffee and remembered something she'd thought of yesterday.

She said to Sam and Dominic ...

"Do you happen to know whether Crites had any property

issues with the Bonnett family before they were killed?"

Dominic said, "No, but we could find out. Sumption Real Estate has been trying to sell that house ever since those murders happened. Somebody there would know."

Bill said, "We should check that out today."

Riley agreed, and the group fell quiet for a few moments.

Then Riley said, "Sam, you mentioned that your father was a cop when the Bonnett family was killed. You said he was part of the investigation."

Sam nodded silently.

Riley said, "Is your father still alive?"

Sam looked somewhat uneasy now.

"Yes," Sam said slowly.

"Could we talk to him?" Riley said.

Sam squinted and said, "Oh, Agent Paige, I don't know. Dad's in an assisted living facility. He's been there for about a year now, ever since my mother died. He's mostly pretty functional, but he's got bad days. He seems to be in the really early stages of dementia. And he gets sometimes gets confused, and he sometimes gets upset. There's nothing that upsets him more than talking about that case. I'm afraid it would be really hard on him."

Riley asked, "Is there anyone else in town who might know as much about the case as he would?"

"I'm afraid not," Sam said.

Riley leaned across the table toward Sam.

"Sam, I understand how you feel," she said. "But if he can remember *anything* that can help us, I really think we should talk to him. I'm asking you, please—can we pay him a visit?"

Sam sighed and said, "Anything to solve this case, I guess. But go easy on him. He's pretty fragile."

Riley and her companions finished eating and left the restaurant. As they had yesterday, the FBI agents followed the local cops in their car. They soon arrived at Hume Place, the assisted care facility where Sam's father lived.

As they walked toward the building, Riley thought it bore an odd resemblance to a typical funeral home. The style of architecture was residential, but the place looked too fake somehow for anyone to actually live there.

Riley's impression didn't change when they went inside the building, with its spacious carpeted foyer and furniture that looked like it had been there for years but even so had barely been used.

Hume Place was obviously not new—there were signs of fairly recent repairs and places where the walls had been repainted. Even so, it struck Riley as a little too clean and spotless and odor-free ...

Like kind of a decayed sterility, Riley thought.

They checked in at the front desk, and Sam led them through the hallways toward her father's room. They were greeted outside the room by a woman in a nurse's uniform.

Riley and her colleagues produced their badges, and Sam introduced the woman as Tracy Spahn, the nurse who took care of her father during this shift.

The nurse looked kindly but agitated.

"Sam, I'm glad you're here," she said. "We were just getting ready to call you."

Sam gasped and grew a little pale.

"What happened, Tracy?" she said. "Is Dad OK?"

Tracy sighed and said, "Yes, he's fine, at least right now, but ..."

She paused, then added, "Sam, you know we try to give our residents as much freedom as possible. This isn't a prison. As long as they're well enough, residents can come and go as they like."

"So what's the problem?" Sam asked.

"Your dad has been going out some nights. Last night, in fact. That's fine, as long as he checks himself out and back in again, and can account for his whereabouts. But lately he's just coming and going without letting anyone know, and he's vague about where he's gone."

Sam looked down and shook her head.

"Oh, dear," she said. "I'm sorry, Tracy. I'll talk to him about that."

"Please do," Tracy said. "Your father has been one of our most independent patients, but he's starting to slip, I'm afraid. He's likely to need more care soon. If he goes out like that again—even once—I'm afraid we'll have to limit his activities, take away some of his privileges. And he's not going to like that."

Tracy opened the door to the room, and Riley and her companions walked inside. It was a small, one-room studio with a kitchen area and a single bed. Sam's father was sitting at a table playing solitaire with a deck of cards.

He smiled a wide smile when he saw his daughter. "Sam—and Dominic, too! It's great to see you! Make yourselves comfortable—you and your friends." Looking at Riley and her colleagues, he said,

"To whom do I owe the pleasure?"

As Tracy sat down at the table with him, she introduced the three FBI agents. Her father exchanged hearty handshakes with Riley and her colleagues and introduced himself as Art Kuehling.

As she, Bill, and Jenn sat down, Riley noted a strong resemblance between father and daughter. Like Sam, Art Kuehling was vigorous and athletic-looking, and his expression was sharp and alert.

He also looked remarkably young for his apparent years. Riley found it hard to believe that he needed to live in this kind of facility.

Then he looked at his daughter affectionately and said ...

"Punkin, it's nice of you to come. But I thought I told you not to—at least not yet."

Sam squinted and asked, "Why not?"

"I just think it's too early to plant tomatoes. Normally this time of year is about right. But there's still a winter chill in the air."

Sam looked shaken.

She said, "Dad, it's August. And you don't have a garden anymore."

Her father tilted his head in mild surprise.

"Oh, is that right?" he said. "Yeah, now that I think of it, I guess I don't."

Sam reached over and took her father's hand.

She said, "Dad, Tracy tells me you're going out at night."

Art chuckled a little and said, "Sure. Is there anything wrong with that?"

Sam said, "You're supposed to check out before you leave, and check in when you come back."

Art shrugged and said, "I always do."

"No, you haven't been doing that, at least not lately," Sam said in a gentle but urgent voice. "Tracy just told me. You've got to follow the rules, Dad."

Art looked a little worried now.

"I guess it's been slipping my mind," he said. "I'll do better."

Sam asked, "Where have you been going at nights, anyway?"

"Just for short walks," Art said. "When I feel up to it, anyway. In this kind of weather, I usually just like to sit out on the back porch swing."

Riley could see Sam gulp hard with emotion.

Her father gazed into her eyes for a moment and said ...

"We don't have that old porch swing anymore, do we?"

"No, Dad," Sam said. "You don't even live in that house anymore."

Art stared silently at the playing cards on the table in front of him.

In a slightly choked voice, he said …

"Sam, I'm afraid I'm …"

His voice faded away and Sam said nothing.

Riley remembered what Sam had said back at the diner …

"He's mostly pretty functional, but he's got bad days."

Riley sensed that this was an especially bad day—probably a lot worse than Sam had expected.

Art pulled himself up and spoke to Riley and her colleagues in a strong, clear voice.

"Well, I don't guess you FBI folks are here on a pleasure visit. How can I help you? Has this got something to do with what happened to Gareth Ogden? He was a mean old cuss, but I never thought anybody would want to kill him. Especially with a hammer like that. Such an awful thing."

Riley was startled by his sudden display of lucidity.

Art continued, "Sam tells me Chief Crane thinks the killer was just some drifter who's long gone." Then he squeezed his daughter's hand and added, "But you don't think so, do you, Punkin?"

Riley could tell that Sam was struggling to keep her emotions in check.

Sam said, "Dad, these agents want to talk to you because you worked on the Bonnett case."

Art's expression clouded a little.

"Is that right?" he said. "Yeah, I remember you said you thought there might be a connection between what happened to the Bonnetts and how Ogden got killed. But I'm sure they've got nothing to do with each other."

"What do you mean?" Sam asked.

Art shrugged and said, "Well, we've got a surefire suspect in custody for the Bonnett killings. Claude Burns, the drunk who lives next door. You know about that."

Sam wiped away a tear.

She said, "Dad, Mr. Burns was cleared ten years ago. He had a solid alibi. And he's been dead for five or six years now."

Art wrinkled his brow and said, "Oh, yeah. Drank himself to death, didn't he? Everybody saw it coming."

Sam nodded, then she gave Riley and her colleagues an imploring look.

She needs to talk to him alone, Riley realized.

Riley glanced at her colleagues, who seemed to understand. Together with Dominic, they all quietly got up and stepped outside into the hallway.

Riley said to her companions …

"This was a mistake."

Jenn said, "You couldn't have known he'd be like this."

Riley shook her head silently and thought …

I should have known.

Sam warned me.

And now they were losing precious time while a killer was at large.

CHAPTER TWENTY

Riley's thoughts were full of conflicting images as she and her companions stood waiting in the hallway for Sam to come out of her father's room.

Sam and her dad had obviously enjoyed a close relationship, unlike what Riley had experienced with her own father. Art had greeted his daughter warmly. Even when his mind was confused, he'd never been angry with her, much less threatening.

Riley's own father had been cold and angry. The last time Riley had seen him alive, they had actually come to blows. She had let her sister, Wendy, take the responsibility for him when he became ill. Riley had even refused to go to his funeral. Although she knew that her father had helped make her the excellent agent that she had become, Riley's memories of him were never warm.

It was clear that Sam's father was fading, a process that was likely to be slow and painful. But the time that they'd already spent together had been rewarding, and Sam's memories of him would be pleasant.

Finally Sam stepped out of her father's apartment into the hallway. As she pulled the door shut behind her, she burst into tears.

Riley watched as Dominic rushed over to Sam and gave her a hug. Then Sam and Dominic both went over to talk to Nurse Spahn, who was standing a short distance away.

Riley's heart went out to Sam. She also felt terrible that she'd instigated what had just happened.

Sam and the nurse were talking quietly, but Riley could make out a few words that the young officer was tearfully saying.

"Please give him another chance … He'll try to be better … Talk to me before you change anything … We'll work something out."

Riley could easily understand what was going on.

Because of his wanderings and his growing confusion, Sam's father's status at the assisted care facility was coming into question. Sam was surely desperate that he might be moved into a part the building for more dependent residents, where his freedoms would be vastly curtailed.

The nurse nodded sympathetically, and Riley sensed that she was agreeing to Sam's appeals, but ...

It's only a matter of time, Riley thought.

Riley didn't know much about dementia, but she was sure the man she'd just talked to in that room wasn't likely to get better. At least, not for very long periods of time. Riley could only imagine how Sam felt to see her once vigorous, keenly intelligent, and still loving and kindly father slipping away from her.

Finally Sam and Dominic walked back over to Riley and her colleagues. Her face looked determined as she brought her tears under control.

Riley touched Sam on the shoulder and said ...

"Sam, I'm awfully sorry. You surely don't want to keep working today. You can stay here with your dad or Dominic can take you home ..."

"No," Sam said, swallowing one last sob. "Dad doesn't want that. He told me he wants me to keep at it today and not worry about him. And that's what I'm going to do."

Dominic said to Riley and her colleagues, "What should we do now?"

Riley didn't have stop to think. There'd been a place she'd wanted to visit ever since she'd arrived in Rushville.

She said, "Could we go to the house where the Bonnets were killed?"

Sam nodded and said, "We'll need to stop by the real estate agency that handles the property. I'm sure they'll let us see it."

As they walked through the building on their way to their cars, Sam added ...

"At least he didn't get upset when I talked about the Bonnetts. I was afraid he would."

*

There was blood everywhere.

Art Kuehling couldn't shake off his horror.

He had never imagined that human bodies even contained so much blood.

He was looking down at Leona and Cosmo—or at least what was left of them.

Starkly lit by the bedroom ceiling light, their faces were all but unrecognizable. Lumps of brain and fragments of their skulls lay around them on the white sheets amid the blood.

Leona's eyes were closed. Art wondered—had she felt any pain at all, bludgeoned in her sleep like that?

If so, her husband hadn't been so lucky.

His eyes were wide open as he lay sprawled in an awkward position beside Leona.

He'd awakened when he heard the attack on his wife, and he'd put up some slight struggle before he'd succumbed to the same fate.

Art shuddered deeply, then retraced his steps down the hall to another bedroom, where the Bonnett couple's oldest child, Martin, lay—his face more mangled than even his parents' faces were ...

And just one year away from his high school graduation, *Art thought.*

Martin's eyes were closed—like his mother, he hadn't struggled before he'd died.

What might he have been dreaming about just before the first hammer blow hit?

Girls, maybe, *Art thought.*

Or maybe music.

The walls of Martin's room were covered with posters of his favorite musicians—rock 'n' roll and hip-hop, mostly.

After all, Martin had been a typical teenager, much like Art himself had once been.

Art wasn't sure if he could force himself to look again into the last bedroom.

I've got to, *he thought.*

I've got to be strong.

He walked down the hall. The overhead light was still on little Lisa's room.

This was the most jarring sight of all—a sea of pink decor and stuffed animals and princesses, with a horrible island of blood and violence at its center.

Lisa's face was even more horribly mangled than the others.

Poor kid, *Art thought.*

Lisa had been the first to die—and even while she was being murdered, the rest of the family remained blissfully asleep until they died the same way.

Art was shaking all over now.

He'd never in his life imagined such horror ...

Art's eyes snapped open and he found himself staring at the

103

tabletop where he'd left a game of solitaire half-finished.

He was sitting slouched in his chair.

Was it a dream or a memory? he wondered.

Had he dozed off, or was this another of his recent mental lapses, or …

Does it even matter?

He was still shaking all over with horror at the images that had come back to haunt him just now.

It was real, he thought. *Too real.*

When his daughter and Dominic and the FBI agents had been here, he'd managed to talk about the Bonnett killings without betraying his deep, lasting horror.

He'd carried that horror around for years, doing his best to keep it to himself.

And now that his mind was finally going, was the horror going to devour him completely? Was he going to disappear into an endless nightmare of blood and smashed skulls?

Would there be no escape from it?

He remembered trying to comfort poor Sam just now. The poor kid, she'd seemed so distraught about what was happening to him.

He'd said to her …

"Stop worrying about me. I'll be all right. Just get back to work. Catch that killer."

Those had seemed like the right words to say at the time.

But now he wondered—had he made a mistake?

Should he have told Sam to walk away from the case, away from her job, away from everything that had to do with violence and death?

She wouldn't have listened, he told himself.

She was a stubborn girl and always had been, and she was determined to follow her own path in life.

And the path she'd chosen was to follow in his own footsteps.

But she had no idea where that path would surely lead.

The nightmare was only beginning for her.

Art Kuehling was sure of it.

CHAPTER TWENTY ONE

During the drive to the real estate office, Riley couldn't shake off her feelings of guilt. She couldn't get the images out of her mind of the retired and fading cop back in Hume Place and of the young cop in tears.

She was aware that Bill kept glancing at her from the driver's seat as he followed Sam and Dominic in their car.

Seeming to read her thoughts, he said …

"Stop beating yourself up about it. What's happening to Sam's father isn't your fault."

Riley sighed and said, "I know, but I shouldn't have insisted on talking to him."

"So what if you hadn't?" Bill said. "What difference would it have made?"

Jenn added from the back seat, "Riley, Sam visits her dad a lot. She was going to have to deal with this—probably a lot sooner than later. It might even be better this way."

Riley fell silent. Bill and Jenn were right, of course. Perhaps she wouldn't be so upset if she could make any sense of this case.

She felt sure that Gareth Ogden's murderer intended to kill again.

But when?

She hadn't gotten any answers from her visit to Sam's father. She hoped that getting a look at the Bonnett house would be more helpful.

The police car pulled up in front of a realty office in a section of the town's business area that had seen better days. The surviving storefronts there looked both old and old-fashioned—a tailor, a shoe repair shop, a drycleaner, and the like. Many of the other small businesses had been boarded up.

Bill parked their car behind the cops and they got out. The painted sign in the storefront window that said "SUMPTION REALTY" was chipped and faded. From outside, the place looked so decrepit that Riley wondered if maybe they had come to the wrong address. Maybe Sumption Realty was just another of the town's apparently numerous defunct business.

The office was gloomy and stuffy as they walked inside. The few pieces of old furniture needed dusting, and she could even see a cobweb in one corner. The condition of the place was hardly any surprise, now that Riley thought about it …

Real estate isn't exactly thriving in Rushville.

A wizened, somewhat elderly woman was sitting at a desk reading a newspaper. Despite a sign that said NO SMOKING, she was puffing away at a cigarette. A drinking glass and bottle of whiskey were on her desk.

Riley, Bill, and Jenn produced their badges and introduced themselves. The woman took a hard look at Sam and Dominic, who were both in uniform, then just nodded.

She turned back to the agents and let out an irritable growl.

"FBI, huh? Well, I don't guess you're here to buy or rent. What's up?"

Riley said, "Can we speak to whoever is in charge?"

The woman tapped a long ash off her cigarette.

"That would be me," she said. "Carol Sumption. What can I do you for?"

Sam said, "These agents would like to look at the old Bonnett house."

Carol shrugged and said, "Well, I'd ask you why, but I guess you've got your reasons. I don't much care about that place one way or the other. It's owned by the late Cosmo Bonnett's brother, Louis. He lives in Albuquerque, and he lost interest in the property years ago. I'll find you the key."

As she rummaged through a desk drawer, Riley asked a question that had been on her mind for a while now.

"Did Amos Crites ever show any interest in the house?"

Carol snorted and said, "Hell, no. Nobody ever did. It's damned hard to sell any house in this town. It's even harder to sell one where four people got beaten to death with a goddamn hammer."

Then with a rough chuckle she added …

"I can't imagine why."

She found the key and handed it to Riley.

A moment later, Riley and her colleagues were following the local cops' car through town toward the Gulf. The house they were looking for was just a few blocks from the beach.

When they got out of their vehicles, Riley could barely make out the "FOR SALE" sign in the front yard. It was covered with weeds and vines. The whole front yard was overgrown with palmettos and other greenery, and the house was in bad need of paint—although no worse than many of the apparently inhabited houses that Riley could see nearby. As in most of this town, there were no sidewalks and the street was in need of repair.

Riley remembered Carol Sumption mentioning that the present owner had long since lost interest in the place. Apparently so had the Realtor herself. It looked like nobody had taken any care of this house for several years now.

Riley and her four companions pushed through the encroaching brush toward the house. Riley took out the house key as she approached the front door. But as she reached out to use it, she saw that the door was open just a crack.

Riley looked at the others, and she could tell they were all wondering the same thing …

Is somebody in there?

Riley took a closer look and saw that the latch was broken. Someone had forced their way in. She gave the door a gentle push, and it opened.

As she and the others went inside, Riley saw that the interior was in shocking condition. In the hallway across the living room, the ladder that led up to the attic was pulled down. At the bottom of the ladder was what was left of the house's air conditioner unit, which seemed to have been ripped out and thrown down from the attic.

Wide gashes had been torn in the walls, and wallboard and insulation hung in scraps all around them.

Dominic explained, "Copper thieves. They raid a lot of empty houses here in Rushville."

Dominic walked over to a wall and pointed inside a particularly ruined section.

"See?" he said. "They kicked through the drywall and pulled out all the wiring—stripped the whole house, it looks like. They did thousands of dollars of damage—and they probably got away with just a few hundred dollars' worth of copper."

The brazenness of the theft struck Riley as rather breathtaking.

She asked, "But how did they do all this without the neighbors noticing?"

Dominic shrugged and said, "They probably pretty much just hauled off and did it in broad daylight."

Sam added, "These thieves probably just drove up in what

looked like a utility truck. They did all this damage while making themselves look like they were here on legitimate business."

Riley rather doubted that no one in the neighborhood had caught on to what was happening here. She thought it more likely that the neighbors simply hadn't cared what became of this abandoned old house where four innocent people had lost their lives.

Peering around the wreckage, Riley could visualize what a pleasant little home this must once have been. There remained some surviving built-in furnishings, including corner cabinets and shelves and a brick wall with a fireplace and a hearth.

Sam asked Riley eagerly, "So are you going to do it again? Get into the killer's mind, I mean?"

For a moment, Riley felt uncertain.

She asked Sam and Dominic, "Do either of you know anything about what this place looked like when people still lived here?"

"I'm afraid not," Sam said.

"Sam and I were still in our early teens," Dominic added. "We didn't live in this neighborhood, and we barely knew the Bonnetts."

Riley kept looking around, assessing the situation.

It might not be easy to get a sense of the killer, but even so …

It should be possible.

After all, she'd seen crime scene photos of the victims. And she knew the orders of the murders themselves. That meant she could be pretty sure of the route the killer had taken through the house.

Riley took a few long, deep breaths and tried to imagine how the killer had felt, standing where she now was in the living room. Of course it had been late and night and the family was sound asleep but …

How did he get in?

Had he picked the front door lock?

Possibly, Riley thought.

If the bedroom doors had been shut and the air conditioner steadily rumbling, perhaps the killer would have felt confident that none of the Bonnett family would hear him.

Still, it seemed unlikely that the killer would have taken such a risk.

Riley walked out onto the porch pulled the door shut behind her. She turned slowly, looking all around.

Her eyes fell on an outdoor thermometer mounted on the outside doorframe. She peered closely at it and saw that the glass had long since been broken. Following a hunch, she reached for the edges of the thermometer.

The front of the thermometer came loose, and Riley found a key that was still behind it, hanging on a hooked piece of metal. The thermometer was actually a modestly clever little spare key holder.

She felt immediately sure of it …

He used this key.

He'd put it back when he'd finished his horrific deeds, and no one else had even thought to look for it until just now.

As she held the key between her fingers, a palpable sense of the killer's thoughts and feelings rose up in her—a wild mixture of anticipation, fear, dread, and exhilaration.

She put the key in the lock of the broken door and turned it, just as the killer must have done.

It felt as though it was much more than just a key to a door.

It was the key to a terrible moment of the past.

CHAPTER TWENTY TWO

As Riley stepped back through the doorway and into the living room, her companions stood still and quiet, giving her space to move and concentrate. Determined to discover whatever she could about that night, she brought all her thoughts and senses into focus on the mind that had driven the murder of a family.

Soon she began to feel it. The years had not erased the evil that had happened here.

As she had done at the Ogden house, she imagined the weight of the hammer in her hand. But she didn't have the self-assurance she had felt at the other house—not yet. Instead, she faintly sensed that the killer had stood here breathlessly, his heart pounding, wondering …

Can I do this?

Should I just get out of here and never give it another thought?

But something was driving him—some powerful emotion …

Anger, Riley thought.

As Riley's feeling of connection grew more intense, an almost tangible darkness seemed to close in around her.

He felt some sort of cold, fierce fury toward at least one of the people in the Bonnett family—enough to drive him to kill all of them.

Riley wondered—had he known the layout of the house?

Did he know who he would find in each of the rooms?

She wasn't sure.

But she had no doubt about the route he must have taken …

One room at a time, in the order I come to them.

She walked into the hall and edged past the attic ladder, which surely wouldn't have been lowered at the time. Then she opened the first door she came to, which was on the left.

She gasped slightly as she looked around.

Although the room was stripped of furniture and belongings, a glance was enough to see that it had once belonged to a young girl. The tattered wallpaper, gouged with holes by the copper thieves, was all pink and painted with princesses and cheerful characters from animated cartoons.

Riley remembered enough details from the crime scene photo to know exactly where the bed had been. She felt a pang of horror well up as she imagined what the killer had thought as he stood in the doorway looking at the peacefully sleeping ten-year-old girl …

Poor Lisa.

She never did anything wrong.

Does she deserve this?

But then, Riley thought, a renewed sense of anger kicked in.

The very fact that the girl was innocent of whatever grievance the man held against the Bonnetts was all the more reason for him to kill her.

Perhaps this would be his only murder.

Maybe he'd let the others live.

Of course, Lisa's death would break the others' hearts. And at least one of their hearts thoroughly deserved to be broken.

Following his footsteps, Riley walked over to where he must have stood looking down at the girl.

Now she felt fully connected with the killer's thoughts and actions …

Looking down at the sleeping child he thought …

I don't dare hesitate.

Without another moment's wavering, he lifted the hammer and slammed it into the child's skull. The girl made a horrible croaking sound, and her whole body twitched violently.

I've got to finish it.

He brought the hammer down again and again until her face was an unrecognizable pulp and her body fell still.

The killer was gasping for breath now …

Keep quiet.

Don't wake the others.

As he slowed his breathing, an eerie calm settled over him—and a twisted sense of pride. He'd just carried out the most appalling and irrevocable act of his entire life. It had taken astonishing fortitude and determination and …

Courage.

Yes, there was something positively heroic about what he'd done.

But should I stop here?

He could just walk out of here, leaving the rest of the family to awaken to the horrible scene of the girl's ghastly murder.

But no—he'd gotten a taste for it now, he lusted for further carnage.

He crept out of the bedroom toward the next door, which was on the opposite side of the hall. He opened the door and found himself looking at the teenaged boy, Martin, who was sleeping as soundly and unwarily as his younger sister had been.

This time he felt no pangs of guilt or conscience—only exhilaration.

The hammer came up, then down again.

Like his sister, Martin made a hideous groaning sound and twitched violently.

Swiftly and surely, the killer slammed Martin's head with the hammer repeatedly.

In another moment, the body lay stiff and still.

The killer could hardly believe his success ...

It's easy!

And it feels so, so good!

He was filled with wild, drunken joy and wanted to shout out loud.

Don't, he told himself.

Keep control.

This was going so well, the last thing he wanted was to botch it.

Again he wondered—should he stop now?

Were the two children's deaths enough?

It would be a fine enough vengeance if the parents simply had to live with their loss.

It would certainly fulfill the killer's purpose.

And yet the mayhem was working inside him like a powerful drug ...

I can't stop now. I don't want to stop.

It was all he could do to keep from breaking into a wild run to his next victims. He sternly reminded himself ...

Keep quiet.

And don't rush.

He crept out of the boy's room and headed across the hall to the last bedroom.

He pushed the door open and saw the couple lying in bed asleep.

It started to dawn on him ...

This will be more difficult.

He walked silently to the bed until he stood at the side where the wife was sleeping.

He knew he couldn't kill either one of them without awakening the other.

He decided to kill the wife first, then keep the husband from escaping.

He hit the woman's head once, and again her body twitched and writhed.

The husband lay facing away from her and didn't awaken immediately.

Instead, he groaned with irritation in his sleep.

Perfect, *the killer thought, landing a couple more hammer blows to the woman's head. Then the husband pitched over toward him, suddenly wide awake and horror-stricken.*

The killer was pleased by the man's horror.

But there was no time to think now.

The killer climbed up onto the bed over the wife's body, pushed the husband onto his back with one hand, then lifted the hammer with the other and brought it down again and again.

When at last he got back to his feet and looked down at his handiwork, he let out a yelp of triumph.

But hardly had the sound escaped his lips before a strange new feeling came over him.

The wild exhilaration gave way to ...

Emptiness.

It was done now.

There was no one else to kill.

It can't be, *he thought.*

It can't be the end.

How could he live the rest of his life without experiencing this intoxication ever again? And besides ...

I could do it better.

I could do it with more skill.

I could do it cleaner and faster ...

The sense of the killer's presence ebbed away, and Riley found herself standing in the empty bedroom staring at torn-up walls.

She stood there gasping for breath.

The experience had been unusually vivid—so much so that she had to remind herself ...

It's all speculation.

I don't know what he really felt.

I can only imagine.

113

Still, the scenario she'd played out in her mind had felt real and it seemed entirely plausible. Even more importantly, what she had experienced here supported the insight she'd had about the recent hammer murder.

She walked back out into the living room, where the two young cops and her FBI colleagues stood waiting for her.

Riley said to them …

"It's just as I thought when we were at the scene of Gareth Ogden's death. There's a definite connection between these killings. Ogden's murder was a sort of a …"

She paused to think of the right word.

"Continuation," she said.

Her companions exchanged slightly confused glances.

Then Jenn asked, "Does that mean we're dealing with the same killer as before?"

Riley hesitated for a long moment.

Then she said, "Yes."

CHAPTER TWENTY THREE

Blaine felt uneasy as he approached Riley's townhouse in his SUV.

He was driving his own daughter, Crystal, and Riley's daughters, April and Jilly, home from school.

The girls are so quiet, he thought.

Again.

Riley had called Blaine yesterday morning to let him know she was on her way to Mississippi to work on a case, and as usual she didn't know how long she'd be away. Blaine knew that April and Jilly usually took the bus to and from school, just like Crystal did. He'd offered to drive them all to school and back while Riley was gone …

Just to be helpful.

He'd thought it would be a nice change for the girls. It had also seemed like an appropriate offer, given the possibility—or was it actually a likelihood?—that he would soon be Riley's daughters' stepfather. And Crystal had certainly seemed excited about the idea.

Blaine had driven them home yesterday afternoon, then to school this morning, and now he was getting ready to drop off Riley's daughters at their house again. At first they had all seemed to appreciate the extra attention and they'd been delighted about not having to ride the school bus home.

But now …

Jilly was sitting in the passenger seat next to him with her arms crossed, sullenly silent. Blaine kept wondering whether he should ask her if anything was wrong.

Or maybe it's none of my business, he thought.

Then again, maybe it *was* his business.

Just how much concern should he start showing toward Riley's daughters?

Meanwhile, April and Crystal were sitting in the seat behind them, and they seemed unusually quiet too. The two girls were in the same grade and about the same age, and the best of friends. Normally they couldn't stop chattering and gossiping and giggling about one thing or another.

When he glanced back in the mirror, Blaine saw that April

looked too preoccupied to be her usual playful self. He guessed that Crystal was respecting April's quiet mood.

Probably also listening to music on ear buds, he thought.

As he pulled the car to a stop in front of Riley's house, he asked Jilly …

"How are things going at school?"

Jilly put her hand on the door handle and said in a barely audible voice …

"Fine."

Blaine finally felt like he had to say something.

"Hold on a minute, Jilly," he said, before she could open the door. "Things don't seem fine. Is there anything you'd like to talk about?"

April leaned over from the back seat and said, "Yeah, I've been wondering too, Jilly. You've been kind of weird lately."

Jilly snapped, "I'll tell you what's wrong. Everybody's getting on my case about everything."

Blaine was shocked by her tone. April sounded shocked as well.

"That's not fair, Jilly," she said. "This is the first time anybody's brought it up."

Jilly's face twitched a little with anger.

"You've been bringing it up a lot."

"OK, maybe I have," April said. "But that's no reason to take it out on Blaine."

"I'm just trying to be helpful," Blaine said.

"I don't need anybody's help," Jilly said.

She opened the door and jumped out of the car and strode toward the house.

Blaine turned off the car engine. He thought maybe he should follow Jilly and talk to her.

Then he heard Crystal's voice …

"Don't bother her, Dad. She'll be OK."

Blaine stayed seated, and April hopped out of the car and dashed after Jilly. As the two girls went into the house, Crystal got into the front seat beside him. Blaine started the car again and pulled away.

After about a minute, Crystal said …

"I'm worried about Jilly."

Blaine glanced at his daughter with surprise.

"But you just told me not to bother her," he said. "You said she'd be OK."

Crystal said, "Yeah, well … I'm a little worried, if you want to know the truth. So is April. She's been telling me so. Something's been going on with Jilly ever since we were on vacation together."

"What do you think it is?" Blaine asked.

Crystal shrugged and said, "Dunno. Some kid thing, I guess."

Blaine sighed and said, "Teenagers are complicated."

"You don't know the half of it," Crystal said with a chuckle. "And believe me, you don't want to know."

Blaine laughed as well. He knew his daughter was teasing him, and right now that came as a relief.

Blaine was about to ask Crystal about her own day when she popped her ear buds back in and started listening to music again. She began bouncing slightly to some catchy pop tune.

Blaine didn't feel shut out by the music. He and Crystal had an easy rapport, and he knew she'd talk to him later if he really wanted her to. Even though she went through her share of teenaged angst, Crystal was usually willing to talk with him about it, and that always seemed to help. As far as he knew, she didn't keep many secrets from him.

Blaine likewise tried to keep few secrets from her. He'd talked to her pretty openly about where things were between him and Riley, and she'd seemed happy with the idea of their two families joining into one.

Jilly will be all right, he told himself, as he continued driving.

But then, some of his own worries started to nag at him.

He hadn't seen Riley at all since they'd all gotten home from the beach a few days ago. That wasn't her fault, of course—he'd been busy catching up on things at the restaurant.

But he remembered how weird it had felt to find Ryan, of all people, waiting at Riley's house for her to come home …

And with his suitcases, no less.

Riley had called Blaine later on to apologize for her ex-husband, and to assure him that Ryan was *not* moving back in, not even temporarily. But she hadn't explained what it was all about.

Blaine prided himself on not being the jealous type. But even so, wasn't it only natural for him to feel uncomfortable about Ryan showing up out of the blue like that?

He remembered what Riley had said when they'd been discussing their future back in the house by the beach …

"I don't think we'll see much of Ryan. And I think that's just as

well."

Things would certainly be better that way.

But was that how things were really going to be?

He glanced again at his daughter, who seemed to be really enjoying her music.

He was sure that Crystal and April had talked all about whatever had gone on with Ryan. Crystal surely knew more about it than Blaine did himself.

Should I just ask her? he wondered.

Then he shook his head and scoffed under his breath ...

How ridiculous.

Was he really going to start asking his daughter about that kind of thing?

Leave it alone, he told himself.

Wherever things were going between him and Riley, he knew they'd both have a lot of adjusting to do, and they'd have to learn each other's boundaries. And he reminded himself that being in a relationship meant living with uncertainties ...

And a few mysteries, too.

He chuckled a little as he thought ...

I'm semi-engaged to an FBI agent, after all.

Mysteries were sure to be part of the package.

*

April sat at the dining room table staring at her laptop, nibbling on an afternoon snack that Gabriela had just made for her. She found it hard to concentrate on homework with an adorable black and white kitten stretched out in in her lap begging to be petted.

April thought wryly ...

Well, it's a price that has to be paid.

She kept on eating with one hand and petting Marbles with the other, not thinking about her homework at all.

Instead, her thoughts turned to the little fight she'd just had with her sister. Jilly had charged upstairs to her room as soon as they'd gotten into the house.

April wished she knew why Jilly was upset now. Just a few weeks ago, she had been so tearfully joyful at being legally adopted and becoming an official part of this family.

She'd seemed to have a good time at the beach. She seemed to like Blaine and Crystal.

So why had Jilly behaved so badly toward Blaine just now?

April wondered if it might be her own fault somehow …

Was it something I said?

As she replayed the scene in her head, she remembered saying to Jilly …

"You've been kind of weird lately."

April shook her head and murmured …

"Weird."

She knew perfectly well that Jilly hated to be called "weird" …

I guess I shouldn't have said that—especially in front of Blaine and Crystal.

Maybe she owed Jilly an apology.

And even if she didn't, maybe just saying she was sorry would help get Jilly to open up about whatever was bothering her.

April looked down at Marbles and said …

"Sorry to do this, girl."

As the kitten let out a mew of protest, April picked her up and set her gently on the floor. Then she walked through the living room and up the stairs. As she entered the hallway, she was surprised to see Jilly's little dog, Darby, curled up on the floor just outside Jilly's bedroom door.

Upon seeing April, Darby looked up at April and whined sadly.

April bent over and petted the dog.

"What's the matter, Darby? Did Jilly leave you all by herself?"

Darby whined again, and April felt a tingle of worry.

Locking Darby out of her room wasn't like Jilly at all.

Something must really be wrong, April thought.

She knocked gently on Jilly's door, but there was no reply.

She guessed Jilly must be listening to music.

She knocked again more sharply, but still got no reply. Finally April turned the doorknob and opened it.

Sure enough, she saw Jilly sitting on the edge of her bed with her ear buds in, completely oblivious to the fact that her sister had just come through the door.

April walked toward the bed to tap Jilly on the shoulder and get her attention.

Then she saw the blood on her sister's leg.

April screamed …

"Jilly! Stop!"

CHAPTER TWENTY FOUR

When Riley's phone buzzed, she was sitting in a fast food place with Jenn and Bill eating burgers and discussing the case. With a tingle of worry, she saw that the call was from April. Her daughter didn't usually call when Riley was at work on a case—at least not without good reason.

Riley took the call and heard April's tearful voice.

"Mom, something's going on with Jilly, she's ..."

April stopped in mid-sentence. Riley's imagination went into overdrive.

Did she run away?

Did she do something else crazy?

Riley got up from the table and walked away from her colleagues so she could talk more privately.

"What?" Riley said breathlessly. "What about Jilly?"

She heard April inhale sharply, then say ...

"Jilly has been *cutting*."

Riley was suddenly confused.

"Cutting?" she asked April. "What do you mean, cutting?"

April sounded impatient now as well as distraught.

"Mom, you *know* what cutting is."

Riley felt like her heart had jumped up in her throat. Of course, she *had* heard of cutting. She knew that teenagers—especially girls—sometimes deliberately cut themselves. But she had never imagined that one of her own daughters would do it.

She struggled with her voice for a moment.

Finally she asked April, "How do you know?"

"I walked in on her, caught her doing it in her room. She was using a really sharp matte knife she got out of our toolbox. She was cutting her thigh, up where her clothes would cover it and we couldn't see it. She's got a bunch of other fresh-looking wounds that are scabbed over."

Riley could hardly believe her ears.

She said, "Put Jilly on the phone. I need to talk to her."

April stammered, "I—I can't do that, Mom."

"Why not?"

"I promised her I wouldn't tell anybody, especially not you."

It was all Riley could do to keep from shouting.

"Why did you do that?" she asked.

"Look, I had to say that, OK?" April said. "She was already having a fit about my coming in and catching her. So I lied and said I wouldn't tell. Then I went right ahead and told Gabriela, and now I'm calling you."

Riley was pacing nervously.

She asked, "Where is Jilly right now?"

"She's in her room. She says she doesn't want to see or talk to anybody."

Riley felt as though her head was about to explode.

What should I do? she wondered.

Then she heard Gabriela's voice as she snatched the phone away from April.

"Señora Riley, this is very serious. The girl needs her mother."

"I—I know," Riley said, her thoughts racing.

"Vente a casa," Gabriela snapped, her voice shaking. *"¡Ya!"*

Gabriela abruptly ended the call. Riley knew what her housekeeper had just said in Spanish …

"Come home—right now!"

Riley stood staring at the phone. Gabriela had sounded both distressed and angry.

But who was she angry with? Jilly, April, herself, or … ?

Me?

Riley quickly realized …

She's mad at all of us.

And Riley was starting to feel the same way.

She remembered noticing a small cut on Jilly's forearm before they'd gone on vacation. Jilly had said that April's cat had scratched her. Riley also remembered what Jilly had said about a similar cut on her thigh when they'd been at the house by the beach …

"Just got clumsy, I guess. Bumped it into a thorn or something else kind of sharp."

Riley fought down a groan of anger and despair.

I should have known, she thought. *We all should have known.*

Riley walked back to the table and shakily sat back down with Bill and Jenn.

She didn't say anything right away.

So much has changed so quickly, she thought.

Just a few moments ago, the three of them had been in deep conversation about the case. After their visit to the Bonnetts' house, Riley, Bill, and Jenn had gone around knocking on doors asking the neighbors about what had happened there ten years before. After hours of fruitless interviews, the three of them came here to get something to eat and decide what to do next.

Meanwhile, Sam and Dominic had checked on the whereabouts of Amos Crites, and they'd called Riley to tell her he didn't seem to be up to anything sinister. They were now back on the waterfront drive, talking again to some of Gareth Ogden's neighbors.

While Riley sat there trying to think of what to say, Bill asked bluntly, "What happened?"

Riley saw that both her colleagues' faces were full of concern.

She gulped hard and said …

"That was April on the phone. She says that Jilly is … cutting herself."

Jenn gasped aloud and said, "Cutting! Oh my God, Riley— that's really serious."

Riley nodded.

Bill said, "You've got to get back to Fredericksburg right now."

"But how can I do that?" Riley said.

"Simple," Jenn said. "We'll drive you to Biloxi, and you'll catch a flight back to Virginia. You can come back as soon as you fix things up at home. You'll probably be back here tomorrow. Bill and I can handle things till then."

Riley said, "But we're in the middle of a murder case. Meredith's still mad at me for not coming down to Rushville when he first suggested it. He'll never give me permission—"

Jenn interrupted. "Riley, look at me."

Riley met Jenn's gaze. Jenn was sending her a wordless message with her eyes—that she'd cover for Riley, no matter what. Riley then looked at Bill and saw the same expression on his face.

She felt a strange mixture of gratitude and guilt.

She knew she shouldn't be surprised that her partners would support her like this. All three of them had covered for each other in similar situations.

I guess that's just our style, she thought.

Always bending the rules.

122

Bill and Jenn drove Riley straight to the airport in Biloxi, where she checked in for connecting flights to the Shannon Airport near Fredericksburg. While she waited at the gate for her plane to board, she tried to clear her head and wondered …

Am I maybe overreacting?

Was it even possible that she'd do more harm than good by rushing home like this?

She doubted it, but she felt like she needed advice from someone who understood such things much better than she did.

She quickly realized who she ought to talk to …

Mike Nevins.

Mike was a forensic psychologist in D.C. who worked as an independent consultant on some FBI cases. He'd helped Riley a lot over the years—not just on murder cases, but with more personal matters, including her bouts with PTSD. He'd become a close and trusted friend.

She dialed his direct number and was relieved not to get his answering machine. Of course he guessed right away that she hadn't called for a friendly chat.

"Riley, what's wrong?" he asked.

Riley immediately felt comforted by his smooth and soothing baritone. She could picture the dapper, meticulous man sitting in his office wearing an expensive shirt with a vest.

She said, "Mike, I'm in Mississippi …"

She paused, not sure what to say next.

Mike said, "Yes, I heard you're working on that murder case down there. Any idea whether you're dealing with a serial or not?"

"Not yet, but …"

She paused again, then blurted …

"Mike, I'm calling about my daughter Jilly. You know, the girl I just adopted. She's cutting herself."

"My Lord," Mike muttered.

Riley continued, "My older daughter called me about it just now. I'm at the airport waiting for the next flight home. But I don't really know what I'm doing. And I'm wondering if I really should—"

Mike gently interrupted, "Yes, you *should* get back home right away, in case that's what you're wondering. This is something you should deal with right away."

Riley realized she was on the verge of tears.

"Mike, I'm just so scared. How serious is this? How dangerous?"

"You mustn't panic," Mike said. "I'm not a pediatric therapist, but I know a little about cutting. I'm sure your daughter isn't suicidal. It's not even about trying to get attention, because I'm sure she didn't want you to find out about it. She was making the cuts where they wouldn't be noticed, I assume."

"That's right," Riley said, swallowing down a sob. "But Mike, I don't understand. Why would she do something like this?"

Mike fell silent for a moment.

"Riley, I don't suppose this is something you want to hear, but teenaged girls typically do hurtful things to themselves out of feelings of unworthiness, low self-esteem. They inflict physical pain on themselves to escape emotional pain."

Riley had no idea what to say now. She was struggling with a mass of terrible, confusing emotions.

Mike continued, "From what you've told me, bringing Jilly into your life has been a rocky business from the start."

"Oh, yes," Riley said in a choked voice.

She flashed back to the first time she'd ever seen Jilly—hiding in a truck cab in the parking lot of an Arizona truck stop, hoping to sell her body to the truck's owner. Living with her father had gotten so desperate, Jilly had thought that a life of prostitution would be better. Riley sometimes thought it was a miracle that she'd been there to save Jilly at that fateful moment.

And of course the adoption had been traumatic for everybody involved. Jilly's father had even tried to kidnap Jilly after the courtroom hearing that made the adoption final.

Mike said, "You've made sacrifices for her—you and April and maybe others who've tried to help."

Like Gabriela, Riley thought.

Mike added, "There's a good possibility that she's feeling guilty about all that. She might well think others have suffered too much on her account, and she's been a burden to all of you and doesn't deserve your kindness."

A tear fell down Riley's cheek.

"She's not a burden," she said. "She's my daughter. And she's April's sister. April feels the same way about her."

"I know," Mike said. "And what I'm suggesting is just one

possibility. But it's a strong one. In any case you need to tell her face to face what you've just expressed to me."

Mike continued talking to her for a few minutes, giving her useful and reassuring advice. He also offered to get in touch Leslie Sloat, a pediatric therapist he had once recommended when April had been going through an especially traumatic ordeal. He promised to make sure Leslie would see Jilly the very next morning.

When the call ended, Riley found herself musing upon her life …

Or rather my lives.

After all, she seemed to live two of them.

In one of those lives, her job was to stop vicious murderers. Right now she was hunting down a psychopath who bludgeoned his victims to death with a hammer, and who would undoubtedly keep on doing so if he wasn't brought to justice.

In her other life, she was a mother of children who needed her love and attention. And right now, one of those children was a fourteen-year-old-girl in such despair that she was inflicting small but painful injuries upon herself.

She thought …

Two lives—so different, impossible to compare.

What would some stranger think of my two lives?

Which situation would seem more dire to someone looking at those lives from outside? Surely most people would consider murder a much more serious matter than a teenaged girl's inner torment …

But not me.

At this moment, the slow torture that Jilly was inflicting on herself seemed as terrible to Riley as any evil she'd ever encountered.

She took no comfort from Mike's assurance that Jilly wasn't suicidal.

For one thing, she didn't quite believe it.

An old adage came into her mind …

"… death by a thousand cuts."

That was what Jilly was really seeking—a long, slow death.

And Riley couldn't allow her suffering to continue even a moment longer than could be helped.

As Riley was in the midst of these thoughts, she heard the announcement that her flight was boarding. She got up and headed for her plane.

*

It was dark by the time Riley's flight landed at the Shannon Airport. She rented a car and drove the short distance home. When she walked through the door, April and Gabriela rushed to meet her.

"Where's Jilly?" Riley asked them.

"Still in her room," Gabriela said.

April added, "She's only come out once or twice to use the bathroom. So are you going to talk to her right now?"

Riley almost said the obvious answer …

"Yes, of course."

But she paused and looked carefully at her sixteen-year-old daughter and her stout, devoted Guatemalan housekeeper. Both of their faces were full of warmth and love and concern.

We're family, Riley thought.

She said, "We *all* need to talk to her. Come on."

Followed by April and Gabriela, Riley went up the stairs and knocked on Jilly's bedroom door.

CHAPTER TWENTY FIVE

The first time Riley knocked on Jilly's door, she received no reply. She glanced back at April and Gabriela then knocked again.

This time Jilly's voice called out …

"Leave me alone."

Riley's anxiety was rising by the second.

This isn't going to be easy, she thought.

She called through the door, "This is your mother."

After a short silence, she heard Jilly say …

"You can come in."

As Riley opened the door and stepped inside, she saw that Jilly was sitting in bed with her computer open on her lap. Her little dog, Darby, was lying sleepily beside her.

Jilly looked at her with surprise.

"Mom—what are you doing home?" she asked.

Then Jilly gasped aloud when she saw Gabriela and April follow Riley inside.

For a moment, Jilly stared at all three of her visitors with an expression of hurt and betrayal.

Then she burst into tears and said, "Oh, April … you promised not to tell Mom …"

April put her hands on her hips and said, "Yeah, well, I lied. What did you expect me to do? Deal with it."

Everybody was quiet for a moment.

Then, to Riley's relief, Jilly chuckled through her tears at April's retort.

Riley could feel the tension in the room break as she, April, and Gabriela all laughed a little as well.

Riley sat down on the bed beside Jilly and said …

"I want you to show me."

"Show you what?" Jilly blubbered.

"You know," Riley said.

Jilly was wearing her nightgown. She pulled the covers down and pulled up her gown and showed Riley the cuts she'd been making on the inside of her upper thigh.

Riley was shocked by the number and depth of those wounds—

almost as shocked, it seemed to her, as she might be by the scene of some grisly murder …

Maybe more shocked.

She was used to death and violence. She wasn't used to this. She felt a stabbing pain deep inside …

Like I'm getting cut too.

There were six wounds in all, the freshest one just barely scabbed over. Others were red and looked like they might be infected.

Gabriela looked down at Jilly's cuts and shook her head.

"¡Dios mío!" she said. "I must get something to take care of those!"

Gabriela hurried out of the room.

Tears were still running down Jilly's face as she said to Riley, "I suppose you want me to tell you—why."

"Do you think you can do that?" Riley asked.

Jilly shook her head no, but Riley thought …

It doesn't matter.

She felt like she had a pretty good idea already, after her conversation with Mike …

Guilt.

Riley looked into Jilly's big dark eyes and gently stroked her hair.

"It's hard, isn't it?" she said. "Adjusting to this new life, I mean."

Jilly shook her head and said, "But I *love* this life. And I love all of you. You're all so good to me."

Riley smiled and said, "That's exactly what I mean. You get nothing but love here. Even when you and April get into a fight, or Gabriela and I scold you, it's always out of love. You're not used to it. It's only been—what?—about a year since I first met you? I'll bet it's quite a shock to your system."

Jilly took a long breath, "Yeah, I guess it kind of is. I mean, my own dad hated me. And he was all I had back then. And now I've got this … and all of you …"

She shrugged and added, "Well, it's all so different."

Riley looked at April, who was standing beside the bed now. With her eyes, Riley silently suggested that April say something.

April said, "Well, we *do* love you. You're such an amazing girl. I mean, just think of how much you've done since you came to live with us. You're smart, you're generous, you're doing great in

128

school, you keep learning all kinds of new things, and you've made lots of friends."

Gabriela had just come back into the room with a first aid kit.

"And you are brave, *chica*," Gabriela added as she opened the box and started tending to Jilly's wounds. "*Muy valiente*. Not everybody has the courage to start life all over again. People give up when it gets hard. But not you. You just keep on going."

"Gabriela's right," April added. "We *more* than love you, kid. I've got to admit we actually *admire* you."

Jilly burst into sobs as Riley leaned over and wrapped her arms around her youngest daughter. She was glad she'd brought Gabriela and April to Jilly's room. They were both saying exactly the things that Jilly really needed to hear.

But now, as Jilly's mother, Riley felt that she had to say something that might hurt her feelings again—at least for a moment.

She hesitated. Jilly seemed to be shaking off her feelings of guilt, and Riley didn't want to stir them up again.

Even so, she said, "Jilly, you might not realize this ... but when you hurt yourself, you're also hurting the people who love you. You're hurting all of us."

Jilly nodded stoically through her tears.

"I guess I know that now," she said.

Riley was struck by how readily—and bravely—Jilly absorbed her words ...

Gabriela was right ... "muy valiente," indeed.

Then April said, "What you've got to do, for all of us, is try to see yourself like we see you—as amazing and strong and ... well, completely lovable. Do you think you can do that?"

Jilly stammered, "I—I'll try."

"You do that," Gabriela said with a sly smile. "Who knows? You might even get to like it."

Jilly's little dog, who had been crouched anxiously on the bed during the conversation, let out a little yap.

April laughed and said, "You hear that? Darby agrees with everything we're saying, and she's absolutely crazy about you. If you just try to see yourself like your dog sees you, you'll have it made."

Everybody in the room laughed, including Jilly. She hugged Darby, who wriggled with affection and licked her face.

Stroking Jilly's hair again, Riley said, "Now I hope you

understand—you'll need some help to deal with all this, and not just from the three of us. You're going to have to spend some time in therapy."

April said to Riley, "By the way, Dr. Sloat called earlier. She said you'd told Dr. Nevins to call her. I went right ahead and made an appointment for Jilly tomorrow afternoon. I hope that's OK."

"Of course that's OK," Riley said, proud of April for taking that initiative.

Then April said to Jilly, "You know, I went to Dr. Sloat when I had my own troubles. You'll really like her. She'll help you get better. She's funny, too—she'll make you laugh."

"That'll be great," Jilly said.

Gabriela finished disinfecting and bandaging Jilly's cuts. Then Riley, Gabriela, and April exchanged hugs with Jilly. April offered to spend the night in Jilly's room, but Jilly insisted that she'd be fine alone. As the group got ready to leave, Jilly asked Riley …

"Mom, could we talk alone for just a minute?"

Riley gulped and nodded, feeling a renewed surge of worry.

What does she want to tell me? she wondered.

Gabriela and April left the room and shut the door behind them. Riley remained sitting beside Jilly on the bed. Jilly sat in silence for a moment, her forehead crinkled in thought.

Finally she said …

"Mom, I want you to tell me about the case you're working on."

Riley sighed and said, "Oh, Jilly, that's nothing for you to worry about."

"Just tell me," Jilly insisted. "I really want to know."

It seemed like an odd request, but Riley explained what was going on in Mississippi—how a recent murder might well be the work of a serial killer, and how this killing might be somehow connected to the murder of a whole family ten years ago.

She also expressed her frustrations with how the case was going.

Surprised at how openly she was talking about it, Riley said …

"I keep getting these *feelings,* Jilly. Like I understand the killer. That's kind of my thing, you know—getting into a killer's head. And I *think*—I'm almost sure—he's the same killer who murdered that family all those years ago. But we just haven't been able to find any evidence. Not yet. And I'm worried …"

Her voice trailed away, and she couldn't bring herself to say the words …

"I'm worried he might kill again before we catch him."

Jilly squeezed her mother's hand and said …

"Mom, I'm really sorry you felt like you had to come home."

Riley shook her head and said, "Jilly, don't *ever* be sorry about—"

Jilly gently interrupted.

"Mom, don't say anything. Especially not that I'm more important than your work, or your family comes before your work."

Riley gazed into Jilly's eyes, startled by the sound of maturity in her voice.

She found herself thinking …

Isn't that how I'm supposed to feel?

That family is more important than anything?

Jilly stammered a little …

"I—I'm not sure what I'm trying to say, but … when you're catching bad guys, you're also being a good mom. At least as far as I'm concerned. And I think April feels the same way. It's especially important to me, though. I haven't been around a lot of … well, goodness in my life. So it's not like you've got two different lives. It's all the same thing."

Riley was startled.

She remembered thinking a while ago that she *did* have two lives—or at least she often felt like it.

Had she been wrong?

Was Jilly right?

Jilly continued, "I guess what I mean is, you're a hero, and you're a mom. You're a *hero* right here and now, helping me with these stupid cuts. And you're a *mom* when you make sure that the world is a safer place to live in. There's no real difference. April and I need for you to keep catching bad guys out there as much as we sometimes need you right here."

For a moment, Riley didn't know what to say.

Then she remembered something Ryan had said to her when she'd driven him home …

"Your life is all of a piece."

And he'd said he admired her for it.

Suddenly Riley felt that she understood things in a way she seldom did.

Jilly shrugged and added, "I guess that doesn't make sense."

Riley hugged Jilly again and said, "It makes all kinds of sense,

Jilly. And thank you for telling me that. It's exactly what I needed to hear right now."

Jilly let out a long yawn and said, "I'm really glad, Mom. Because I'm too tired to talk anymore."

Jilly curled up in Riley's arms and promptly went to sleep.

*

Both April and Gabriela had gone to their own rooms by the time Riley left Jilly's room. She went downstairs and got a snack, then went to her bedroom and got ready for bed.

Checking her phone one last time, she noticed that Bill had sent her a text message …

Hope things are OK. Let me know.

Riley punched in Bill's phone number, and he answered. She told him that things were a lot better with Jilly now.

She heard Bill breathe a sigh of relief.

"I'm glad to hear that," he said.

Riley felt touched that he cared so much about her home life. But she guessed that was part of what Jilly had been trying to tell her—and what Ryan had been saying as well …

All of a piece.

Bill wasn't just a colleague. He was like part of her family.

And so was Jenn.

Riley said to Bill, "I take it you and Jenn haven't had any breaks in the case."

"Not a thing," Bill said, and then went on to describe their routine, unproductive activities.

Then he said, "Riley, I've been thinking … if you're right, and Ogden's killer was the same person who murdered the Bonnetts, he really might be done killing for a while. Maybe it will be another whole decade before he kills again—if he ever does."

Riley fell quiet. She felt differently, but she knew perfectly well Bill might be right.

She then explained that she already had plane reservations for tomorrow, and she told him the time in the afternoon when he and Jenn could pick her up in Biloxi.

Then they ended the call, and Riley lay down in her bed.

It had been a strange, tiring day, and she quickly started to drift off to sleep.

As wakefulness faded, she worried about the killer.

If Bill was right and he was through killing for the time being, might he disappear altogether, just as he had since the Bonnett killings?

We can't let that happen.

We just can't.

She wondered where he was at that very moment.

Like her, was he starting to fall asleep?

If so, what would he dream tonight?

And if not ...

What is he thinking?

What is he doing right now?

CHAPTER TWENTY SIX

Vanessa Pinker came out of the restroom and walked through the movie theater lobby. When she reached the glass doors leading outside, she just stood there and stared out into the almost-empty parking lot, watching the handful of other moviegoers heading for their cars.

She sighed and thought …

Do I really want to go out there?

She'd just spent two hours watching an unmemorable romantic comedy in air-conditioned comfort. Actually, it had been just a little too chilly in the theater, and she'd half-wished she'd brought along a sweater. It was cool here in the lobby as well. But she knew she was in for a rude shock when she walked outside.

Just a minute or two more, she thought.

I've got to enjoy it while I've got it.

The air conditioning in her car had broken down, and the cooling system at home was on the fritz. Her husband, Reid, claimed to have fixed it, but of course he hadn't done anything of the kind.

One would think being married to a school custodian would have its advantages, she thought.

But Reid was just plain incompetent when it came to household chores.

When she'd left home a while ago, Reid had been sprawled in front of the TV watching a football game while enjoying his beer and pretzels, seemingly oblivious to the hot, sticky discomfort.

He also hadn't cared that she wanted to get out and go to a movie, and that was just as well. Vanessa had felt like she would gnaw off a leg to get away from him tonight. She'd felt the same way about their two kids, who'd really been at their worst all summer.

Tad had been teasing little Becky about Gareth Ogden's murder ten days ago.

"The Carpenter's going to get you!" he'd kept telling her. *"Soon as you go to sleep, he'll beat your head in with his hammer!"*

134

"Will not!" Becky had wailed through her tears.

"Will so!"

"How do you know?"

"Because he told me so," Tad had said with a sneer, *"'Becky's next,' he told me."*

Vanessa had scolded Tad and tried to comfort Becky. But Tad just kept right on teasing, and Becky was a hopeless wreck, whining and crying. Sometimes Vanessa wondered what was wrong with that girl—the way she cried about everything and seemed to be scared of her own shadow.

Was she ever going to snap out of it?

If not, how was she going to get through life like that?

Of course, Reid had been no help with the kids through all this. He'd just ignored them and popped open another beer.

Vanessa had been pretty gruff with the kids, and she felt a little guilty about that. After all, there was really nothing for them to do when school was out. It was too hot even to enjoy the beach. This town didn't offer anything else and neither she nor Reid had been up for driving them to Biloxi or anyplace else to find entertainment.

She sighed again …

This weather brings out the worst in everybody.

As she watched the handful of cars start to drive away, she thought …

It's now or never.

She opened the door and stepped out into the suffocating blast of heat. She glanced at her watch and saw that it was after nine. Had it gotten any cooler at all since she'd left the house? Was the night going to bring any relief?

Probably not, she thought.

The chances of her getting a good night's sleep were just about nil.

As Vanessa walked toward her car, she glanced back at the movie theater. Except for posters to advertise the movie she'd just seen, its displays were empty. The old multiplex had four screens but was only showing the one movie.

Pathetic, she thought.

There had been talk lately about the multiplex going out of business. It would leave Rushville without any movie theaters at all, but Vanessa wondered …

Would it matter?

There seemed to be less and less to do in town every day.

135

People were moving away, and those who stayed seemed so listless and lifeless that they seldom bothered to leave their homes, even when the weather was nicer than this.

Vanessa hadn't parked far away, but now the walk seemed longer than it really was. In this humidity, it felt more like swimming.

As she continued along, she felt an unexpected little stab of fear. *The Carpenter,* she thought, remembering the name that Tad had used to torment poor Becky.

Before Gareth Ogden got killed, she hadn't heard that nickname for …

How long had it been?

Years, I guess.

The Carpenter was what folks had called whoever killed the Bonnett family about ten years ago. Despite the heat, Vanessa felt goose bumps rise at the memory of that unsolved crime—and also a surge of renewed grief and sadness. She'd actually had a teenaged crush on Martin, the older of the two Bonnett kids.

I should have told him I liked him, she thought for the hundred thousandth time.

Even if she couldn't have prevented his death, maybe he would have liked knowing she'd felt that way.

And if she *could* have prevented his death?

Well, maybe things would have worked out between them.

And maybe today Vanessa wouldn't be stuck with a loser for a husband and two impossible children.

She scoffed aloud at herself …

Such a fantasy life I've got!

Meanwhile, the town was abuzz about the new murder. People were talking about the Carpenter again, even though Chief Crane assured everyone that Gareth Ogden's murder was in no way connected with what had happened to the Bonnetts. Crane said this was just the work of some random drifter who had surely fled Rushville that very night.

Still, it was an unsettling thought …

Another murder with a hammer.

She was startled out of her reverie by the sound of footsteps behind her.

Who can that be? she wondered with a shudder.

There had been nobody else in the parking lot. The other moviegoers had already driven away. There were only a couple of other cars parked at the far edge of the lot, and they probably belonged to people who worked at the theater.

Could somebody have popped out of the woods adjoining the parking lot?

Should she look behind her to see who it was?

Somehow she couldn't make herself do that.

Trying to fight down her panic, she ran the short remaining distance to her car. When she got to the door, she fumbled through her purse looking for her keys.

As the footsteps came closer, a man's voice said, "Hey, Vanessa..."

She turned around and gasped with relief at who she saw.

"Oh, it's you!" she said. "You gave me such a scare. But what are you doing here? And why did you have to—?"

Before she could finish her sentence, she saw his raised arm and a flash of steel, and she only had a split second to realize ...

I'm going to die now.

CHAPTER TWENTY SEVEN

Riley's eyes snapped open at the sound of her cell phone buzzing on her nightstand. She let out a groan of despair.

This is not good news, she thought.

She picked up the phone and heard Bill's voice.

"Riley, we've got trouble."

Shaking herself awake, Riley replied, "There's been another murder, hasn't there?"

"That's right. This time it's a housewife. She was alone coming out of a movie theater when it happened. She got killed in the parking lot. A theater employee found the body after the place closed for the night. And it's the same M.O. as the Ogden murder— one swift hammer blow to the forehead."

She heard Bill let out a discouraged sigh.

He said, "Jenn and I are here at the murder scene. So are Chief Crane and a team of local cops, and Sam and Dominic."

Everybody but me, Riley thought.

She could hear a rumble of voices and activity over the phone.

"What about the county ME?" Riley asked.

"He's not here yet, but we're expecting him any minute," Bill said. "Riley, I don't want the body moved until you've had a chance to look at."

Riley understood perfectly. It would be best if she, Bill, and Jenn could all examine the murder scene together in its present state.

But how was she going to get there in time?

Her commercial flight wasn't scheduled until tomorrow afternoon. Keeping the current scene intact during all that time just wasn't going to be feasible, especially not in that terrible heat.

Her thoughts were still foggy from just having been awakened. But she quickly realized that the only way to get to Rushville in time would be on an FBI plane. And that was going to present a serious problem.

She rubbed her eyes and asked, "Have you been in touch with Meredith?"

"Yeah," Bill said slowly.

Riley was about to ask Bill whether he had told Meredith where she was.

But something in the tone of his single-word reply told her …

He's still covering for me.

So is Jenn.

This was a mess for all of them, and Riley knew that the less she and Bill discussed it right now, the better.

Instead she said, "Keep everything as it is. I'll be there as soon as I can."

Riley and Bill ended the call, and she sat staring at the phone for a moment. The next call she had to make was going to be really rough.

She dialed Meredith's direct number and quickly heard the team chief's gruff voice …

"Paige, what's going on down in Rushville? Have you got any leads?"

Riley swallowed hard and said …

"Chief, I'm not in Rushville. I'm at home in Fredericksburg."

An icy silence ensued.

Riley wondered …

Should I try to explain?

But no, she figured there was no point in that. And he probably wouldn't bother asking. What would Brent Meredith care about her family troubles—especially a non-life-threatening crisis with her younger daughter?

Finally Meredith growled, "How long have you been back from Rushville?"

"I just flew back this evening," Riley said.

Meredith said, "Goddamn it, I talked to Agents Jeffreys and Roston—both of them. Neither one of them mentioned that you'd left. But I kind of had a feeling …"

Riley shuddered as another silence fell. Obviously Meredith had sensed her partners' evasion on the phone. She hoped that Bill and Jenn hadn't lied to him outright. But of course if she'd had to cover for either of them …

That's probably what I'd do.

In a sharper voice than before, Meredith said …

"Agent Paige, this isn't acceptable. Not on your part, and not on your partners' either."

"I understand," Riley said.

Meredith then let out a grunt of anger and said, "No, I'm not sure you really do. Agent Paige, you seriously dropped the ball. While you were AWOL, there was another murder."

Riley stifled a gasp and almost exclaimed …

"Chief, that's not fair."

After all, her mere presence in Rushville wouldn't have prevented the killer from striking again. This new death wasn't her fault.

Even so, she knew she fully deserved the blunt of Meredith's wrath.

His voice growing louder, Meredith said, "Paige, I've got half a mind to pull you off the case and call you and your partners back to Quantico. Start fresh with a new team down there. But I can't, because you've already gotten started. And besides …"

Riley sensed that he was about to add, *"You're the best agents I've got."*

But however true that might be, he sure wasn't going to say so right now.

Meredith continued, "I'm ordering a plane to be ready to take you back down there. Get your ass to Quantico immediately."

"I will, sir," Riley said.

"And solve the case. There's going to be hell to pay for all three of you when you get back. It'll be a lot worse if you fail to bring in the killer."

Brent Meredith ended the call.

The phone was shaking in Riley's hand. She almost felt like crying. Meredith had been frustrated and even angry with her before, but she couldn't remember him being this enraged.

And how was this going to end—for her and her colleagues?

Riley herself had been reprimanded, suspended, and even fired plenty of times, but usually by Meredith's own boss, Special Agent in Charge Carl Walder. Whenever she was in trouble with Walder, Meredith usually came to her defense. Besides, Walder was a bumbling opportunist she had no respect for. She respected Meredith tremendously, and it was heartbreaking to feel that she'd let him down.

But right now, she didn't have a minute to lose.

Riley sent a quick message to Bill. Now she had to get dressed, wake up Gabriela and let her know she was leaving, then drive her rented car straight to Quantico to catch that plane.

As she dashed around getting ready, Riley remembered the conversation she'd had with Jilly a little while ago.

"It's not like you've got two different lives," Jilly had said. "It's all the same thing."

She remembered, too, Ryan telling her …

"Your life is all of a piece."

She'd believed that herself before she'd gone to bed.

But now she felt as though she'd awakened again to a grim and familiar reality …

It's no use.

It's all too much.

I'll never be everything I need to be.

CHAPTER TWENTY EIGHT

Riley groped helplessly through the darkness that surrounded her.

Light, *she thought.*

She needed just a glimmer of light to help her with her search ...

... although she couldn't remember exactly what she was searching for.

Holding one hand out in front of her, she took another cautious step.

She had a sudden strong sense that someone was standing in front of her.

"Who's there?" she asked.

She thought it must be a killer. One of the long line of monsters she had faced before.

But why couldn't she tell?

She repeated again ...

"Who's there?"

Then she heard a harsh and familiar laugh.

A voice replied, "Who do you think it is, girl?"

Now Riley could make out a familiar shadow hulking in front of her.

"Daddy?" she said.

"Yep," he said, laughing again. "And dead as usual."

Either the darkness had lifted a little, or her eyes were starting to adjust. She was beginning to see the features on his face and the contours of his full-dress Marine uniform.

Riley's throat tightened with despair.

"Daddy, I feel so confused," she said.

"About what? The case you're working on? Well, just follow your goddamn instincts. Isn't that what you always do? What are your instincts telling you right now?"

Riley struggled to put her thoughts together.

She stammered, "Th-that these two new murders are ... a continuation ..."

"Of what?"

"Of what happened to the Bonnett family."

The shadowy figure shrugged.

"'A continuation,'" he said. "An interesting choice of words. So it seems you're looking for a killer who's been laying low for ten years and has reared his head again. Now that you know that, the rest should be easy. Just find and catch the bastard—before he does it again."

With a grim chuckle he added ...

"No pressure."

The dim figure started to disappear into the dark again.

Riley said, "Daddy, why is it so dark? Why can't I see?"

"It's always dark," her father said. "We just don't notice it most of the time—because we think we can see the truth. We think we know what's what. That's how it is with everybody. Of course, it's a bit different with you. You've got this 'gut feeling' trick going, your celebrated 'instinct.' Maybe it's not quite like being able to see in the dark, but you can get pretty close to the truth at times."

He slipped completely from view, and when he spoke again, he sounded farther away ...

"You've still got a lot to learn, though. For example, you can be right *about something, and* wrong *about it too, both at the same time. Absolutely right, absolutely wrong. That's where you are right now—absolutely right, absolutely wrong. You just haven't figured it out yet."*

Riley's mind reeled ...

What can that possibly mean?

But before she could ask that question aloud, she felt herself falling, as if the ground had dropped out from under her feet ...

Riley jerked wide awake.

"Sorry about that," the pilot's voice came over the intercom. "Be sure you're buckled in. We'll be landing now."

She realized that a sudden slight drop of the FBI plane had awakened her. She wasn't surprised that she'd fallen asleep on the trip back to Mississippi. She'd only had an hour of sleep tonight.

And now she realized ...

I dreamed about Daddy again.

Those dreams were always unsettling, but this one seemed more so than usual. Those words kept rattling in her brain ...

"Absolutely right, absolutely wrong."

For some reason, it seemed weirdly true. But how could that

be? It didn't even make sense.

As she watched the plane's descent through the window, she told herself …

It was only a dream.

*

When Riley arrived at the airport in Biloxi, Jenn was waiting there to drive her straight to Rushville and to the crime scene. They soon pulled into the parking lot and parked in the outside the area cordoned off by police tape.

As they got out of the car, Riley glanced around.

What a mess, she thought.

Gawking townspeople were crowded around outside the taped-off area. There were also three TV news vans with satellite dishes parked nearby. Riley was sure that the media vehicles were from larger towns in the area, not from right here in a little town like Rushville.

Riley said to Jenn, "I should have gotten here sooner, before the media and all these people arrived."

Jenn replied, "It wouldn't have made much difference. They started showing up about as fast as Bill and I and the local law could get here. The cops were barely able to tape off the scene in time to keep them from getting to the body."

"How did they find out so fast?" Riley asked.

Jenn said, "The theater employee who found the body must have started calling people a minute after he called the cops. Word gets around fast in a town like this, even at this hour. Then I guess somebody must have thought it clever to notify TV stations throughout the area."

Riley could imagine phones ringing around town, then people scrambling out of bed and driving straight over to this movie theater that was tucked behind the shopping mall.

Riley glanced toward the multiplex and saw that only one movie was playing there—a recent romantic comedy.

She thought wryly …

I guess people are pretty desperate for entertainment in this one-show town.

The people didn't even seem to mind the suffocating heat that hung over the pavement in the still night air.

As Riley and Jenn approached the police tape, they could hear one of the TV reporters as she spoke to a camera and a boom microphone …

"… so it looks like Rushville's infamous 'Carpenter' killer is back and hard at work. How many more lives will he take before he's through with his murderous rampage?"

Riley growled under her breath. She wanted to charge over to the woman and tell her to shut the hell up and stop stirring up local panic, but …

I'd wind up on TV too.

And the TV news crew would definitely love that. It was best for to stay out of public view for as long as she could.

The two agents pushed through the crowd of people straining to get a glimpse of the scene. Among them, Riley recognized a few faces she'd seen around town. Brandon Hitt was there. His brother, Wyatt, didn't seem to be with him, which was a relief to Riley. She was sure that kid had seen enough dead bodies for a lifetime.

She also saw Amos Crites, who was staring back at her with a scowl on his face.

When she reached the yellow tape. Riley flashed her badge to a tired-looking cop, who lifted the tape so they could pass on through.

Riley saw that the body was fairly well concealed among parked vehicles, including the county coroner's van. She made her way to where the covered body lay on the pavement beside a car that must have belonged to the victim.

The uniformed coroner was standing nearby. So were Bill, Dominic, and Chief Crane. Bill gave Riley a silent, expectant look. But Riley knew that now was definitely not the time to tell him how furious Meredith was with their team.

Crane looked at Riley angrily and said, "It's about time you got here. Coroner Kuchan's been anxious to take away the victim's body."

Fanning his face with his hat, the big, slouching coroner nodded and said …

"I am at that. She was killed around nine fifteen, so she's been in rigor for a while now, and she's not going to get any fresher. Cadavers start going ripe fast in this kind of heat. We need to get her into a cooler as soon as we can."

Then with a wave of his hand, the coroner said to Riley, "Have yourself a look."

Riley knelt down beside the victim, who was lying flat on her back. She gently pulled the sheet away from the victim's face. Sure enough, there was a single small round crater in the center of her forehead. Riley could see that there had been a lot of bleeding. Because of the heat, blood on the woman's face and the surrounding pavement had already turned black.

The woman's eyes were still open, and she stared dully up at the sky with an expression of only mild surprise.

Riley sensed right away …

She knew her attacker.

But she had no idea what he was about to do.

Riley asked, "What was her name?"

Chief Crane said, "Vanessa Pinker, a housewife with a son and a daughter, both of them still kids. I knew her a little—enough to say hi when I ran into her, anyway. A nice lady."

"Where are her husband and kids?" Riley said.

"At home," Crane said. "Her husband, Reid, insisted on coming right over here after a couple of my cops went to their house and gave him the bad news. He didn't stay long. He was a real mess when he left."

I can imagine, Riley thought.

She peered closely at the woman's face. Despite the hubbub going on around her, Riley tried to play out the killer's actions in her mind …

He walked right up behind her as she was about to get into her car after coming out of the movie.

He might have even said her name.

Then she turned around and had just enough time to recognize him before he …

Riley paused, feeling momentarily uncertain.

She reached back into her memories of the previous two murder scenes. At the Bonnett's home, she'd thought she could sense the killer's thoughts after murdering the family of four …

I could do it better.

I could do it with more skill.

I could do it cleaner and faster.

She also remembered sensing his lust for more killing after that slaughter—a craving that might well have built to an unbearable point over the next ten years until it exploded into action a week and half ago.

Now Riley brought back her impressions at the house near the beach, when she'd thought she'd sensed what was going through his head the moment before killing Ogden …

This won't be like last time.
Not so sloppy and reckless.

Looking down at the body now, Riley could imagine the killer gazing down at Vanessa Pinker, watching her body twitch as her life ebbed quickly away, the blood still red and fresh.

It hadn't been personal—at least not this time. He may have known this woman and even stalked her, but first he had chosen her at random.

And she sensed that he felt pleased with what he'd done ...

Or more than just pleased.

The killer was now in the throes of his own gratified aggression. After all those years of dormancy, it was all flowing so easily and effortless now ...

I'm a true master.
There's no need for further delay.

Riley shuddered as the feeling of the killer's thoughts ebbed away.

She rose to her feet and saw Bill, Jenn, Sam, Dominic, and Chief Crane had been standing there watching her.

She said to Chief Crane, "We've got to catch him quickly. He's not going to waste any time before he kills again. He's ready and eager, and he may well have chosen his next victim already. He could be just looking for the right moment to strike."

Crane's mouth dropped open.

"How do you know?"

Riley realized that, unlike Sam and Dominic, Crane was still unfamiliar with this technique of hers. She hoped that Bill and Jenn weren't going to launch into a detailed explanation.

She was relieved when Bill said simply, "Trust her instincts, Chief Crane. Agent Paige is a superior profiler. She knows what she's talking about."

Crane just kept staring at Riley.

She said to Crane, "I hope you understand now—this wasn't just some random drifter who came and went. You've got an active serial killer right here in Rushville. And you'll need our help to stop him."

Crane let out a grunt of dismay.

"Well, I guess this is where I ask for the FBI's help. OK, then. Consider it official."

Then Crane glanced over at the news vehicles.

He said, "Have you heard those damned reporters? 'The

Carpenter is back,' they're saying. The 'Carpenter'—that's what folks used to call whoever killed the Bonnetts. As if this has anything to do with that."

Riley stifled a sigh.

He still doesn't get it, she thought.

Crane just couldn't be persuaded that these new killings were a continuation of what had happened to the Bonnetts.

Still, she understood how he felt about what the reporters were saying. She hated it when killers acquired public nicknames. It always stirred up extra anxiety and fear. It also tended to please the killer, who would start to think of himself as some sort of living legend. Delusions of glory would only make him more eager for the next kill.

Not what we need right now, she thought.

Her thoughts were interrupted by the sound of Dominic's voice …

"Hey, Sam! Get back over here!"

Dominic was calling out to his partner, who had gone over to the crowd behind the yellow tape. She was talking to someone—Brandon Hitt, the newspaper boy's older brother.

At the sound of Dominic's voice, Sam came back over to the group standing around the body.

Dominic looked and sounded angry now.

"What do you think you were you doing over there, Sam?" he asked.

"Just talking to Brandon," Sam said with a shrug. "He waved at me to come over, so I did. He just wanted to ask about the case."

"Like hell," Dominic said. "He was flirting with you."

Sam let out a scoffing sound.

"He was not," she said.

"He was too," Dominic said. "I could see that from all the way over here."

Sam shrugged and said, "So what if he was?"

Riley didn't much care whether the conversation was flirtatious or not. It worried her for other reasons.

She said, "Sam, it's never a good idea to talk to civilians at a crime scene if you can possibly help it."

Sam's eyes widened guiltily.

"Oh, of course it's not," she said. "I'm sorry, I was acting like a dumb rookie. But I didn't tell him anything that he didn't already know—just that there was a new victim."

Riley breathed a little easier. It didn't sound as though the young cop had said anything inappropriate.

But Dominic continued snapping at Sam about her "flirtation," and she kept replying defensively.

For the first time Riley realized …

He's in love with her.

Riley was also sure that Dominic's crush was unrequited.

She felt a little foolish for not picking up on that when she'd first met the pair. All she'd really noticed was that Sam was the smarter partner of the two, and that they seemed to make a good team.

But were they really?

Bickering at a murder scene wasn't a good sign.

Riley was about to tell them both to knock it off when Sam's phone rang and she skulked away to take the call, leaving Dominic to fume silently by himself.

I'll talk to them about this later, she thought.

The last thing this investigation needed was this kind of emotional distraction.

Riley told the coroner to take the body away and watched as his crew lifted the woman onto a gurney. She saw that the coroner was right—the corpse was stiff with rigor mortis. It was definitely time to get it into the morgue.

Then Riley turned toward Bill and Jenn, getting ready to talk to them about how they should proceed.

But before she could say anything, Sam came charging back toward the group, the phone shaking in her hand. Riley was shocked to see that she was in tears.

"Something's happened!" Sam said. "It's my dad."

Sam gulped down a sob, then continued …

"That was Nurse Spahn at Hume Place. She said Dad has disappeared again. They have no idea where he is."

Riley stifled a groan of annoyance.

She almost snapped at Sam …

"We don't have time for this. You can worry about it later."

But as she looked into Sam's eyes, she realized that her panic was deep and real.

She said, "We'll handle things for a while. You and Dominic go ahead and look for your dad."

Sam let out a sob of gratitude. As Sam and Dominic headed away for their police car, Riley thought about Sam's father. She remembered how struck she'd been away how vigorous, athletic, and alert Art Kuehling had seemed. Until they'd talked him for a little while, she'd found it hard to believe that he was slipping slowly into dementia.

Riley almost gasped as she thought …

And now he's out!

It suddenly seemed all too possible that Art Kuehling was the killer they were looking for.

CHAPTER TWENTY NINE

Sam's hands were sweating on the steering wheel as she drove through the streets of Rushville, hoping to catch sight of her father somewhere. She'd been frantic ever since Nurse Spahn had called to tell her that he had gone missing from Hume Place again.

Sitting beside her in the passenger seat, Dominic said …

"Sam, we're driving a long way from the rest home. Why do you think he'd have wandered so far?"

Sam growled, "He's still got a car, Dominic. You know that."

And that's going to change as soon I get him back to the home, she thought.

She'd gotten angry at Nurse Spahn on the phone, and she wished she hadn't.

And yet …

Why didn't anyone tell me sooner?

Following proper protocol this time, her father had checked out of the facility earlier that night. He'd said that he'd be back by midnight. Although Nurse Spahn was his main caregiver there, it wasn't her shift. When Sam's dad didn't show up at midnight, the night nurse hadn't bothered to worry about his absence for an hour or so. It hadn't been until well after midnight before the facility had sent some employees out looking for him. Finally they'd called Nurse Spahn, and she had called Sam.

Sam reminded herself that none of this was Nurse Spahn's fault. But others at Hume Place could have handled things a whole lot better. Sam was still angry as well as panic-stricken.

Dominic said, "Sam, you're a nervous wreck. Maybe I should drive."

Sam thought for a moment …

Maybe he's right.

She'd have been alarmed by her father's disappearance in any case. But the situation seemed especially terrifying on a night when a serial killer had taken yet another victim.

Should she give Dominic the wheel?

She thought for a moment, then made a decision.

"I'll keep driving," she replied.

Sam didn't want to have to think about where they should go looking for Dad and then have to keep telling Dominic. She wanted to follow wherever her own impulses took her. They had already checked out the logical places, and now she would have to depend on her intuitions to find him.

They'd begun by driving by her childhood home. It had been sold a long time ago, and a different family now lived there. The house had been dark, and Sam hadn't been able to bring herself to wake up its inhabitants to ask if an addled old man had been at their door sometime that night.

They also drove by some of her father's old familiar haunts—places like Donnelly's Bar and Rog's Pool Hall. Of course those establishments were closed at these wee hours of the morning. Even so, Sam couldn't help hoping that, in his mental confusion, her father might turn up outside one of those places.

As she turned onto the waterfront drive, she said to Dominic …

"Let's keep our eyes on the beach. He used to like to walk there after dark."

She heard Dominic let out a growl of disapproval.

"Sam, you're letting your imagination run away with you. He's not in any real danger. Sure, he's been slipping out on his own lately, but he always comes back. He'll come back this time too."

Sam felt a sob rise in her throat.

Don't cry, she told herself.

After all, Dominic was surely right. As awful as tonight's murder was, there was surely no danger to the public here in Rushville, at least for the moment. It seemed extremely unlikely that the killer was still stalking the streets right now, looking for another victim so soon. That didn't seem to be his MO.

Still, she couldn't shake off her panic.

It was a clear, moonlit night, and she and Dominic had a good view of the beach from the car. By the time they'd driven the whole length of the drive, they hadn't seen any sign of her father or anybody else walking by the water.

Sam cursed silently to herself. She should have insisted that he get rid of that car as soon as he'd shown telltale signs of mentally slipping. But until very recently, he'd seemed self-sufficient and alert, despite those occasional lapses.

Desperate scenarios were welling up in her mind.

What if he drove out of town?

He might wind up many miles away and have no idea where he

was.

And what if he has a car accident?

As she racked her brain trying to think of where to look next, a name popped into her head …

Tony Appleton.

Tony was another retired cop. Although her dad hadn't mentioned seeing Tony lately, they'd been good buddies when Art was still on the force.

I'll bet that's where Dad is, Sam realized.

At least, it seemed like a strong possibility, and she knew exactly where Tony Appleton lived.

Sam suddenly turned the car so sharply that Dominic let out a small yelp of alarm. She headed back into town and drove straight to the other retired cop's house. Sure enough, there was her father's car, parked in the driveway. The lights were on in the well-kept little home.

Dominic said, "Looks like we've found him."

We sure have, Sam thought, not sure whether she felt relieved or angry.

She parked the car, took out her cell phone, and typed a quick text message to Agent Paige …

Dominic and I found Dad. We'll take him back to Hume Place. Then we can come back to work. Call and tell us where we should meet you. Sorry for running off.

She and Dominic got out of the car and walked up to the house. Sam knocked on the front door, and after a few moments she heard someone stirring inside. Then Tony opened the door . His wrinkled face lit up when he saw who had arrived.

"Well, I'll be damned!" he said. "Hey, Art—look who showed up for our festivities!"

Tony escorted Sam and Dominic inside. She saw her father's back as he sat hunched over a worktable. He turned his head and saw his daughter.

"Hey, Sam!" Art said with a wide grin. "Look what Tony and I've been doing!"

He held up a fluffy and colorful little object in his hand.

Sam quickly realized …

They've been making fishing flies.

Tony sat back down at the table with Sam's dad, sipping on a

153

bottle of beer. A half-empty beer bottle was within her dad's reach. Sam looked around and saw only two other empty bottles in the whole room.

At least they're not drunk, she thought.

In a shaky voice she asked, "Dad, you've had me scared half to death. How long have you been here?"

Her dad hesitated for a few moments. He wrinkled his brow and stammered, "I—I'm not quite sure."

Tony shrugged and said, "Since around eleven. Is there some kind of problem?"

Sam groaned aloud at Tony's question …

Where do I even begin?

*

The three FBI agents were pulling into the parking lot at Hume Place when Riley took out her phone and saw Sam's text message. She breathed a sigh of relief that Sam had found her father.

At least we know where he is. And she's bringing him here.

Riley briefly considered calling Sam back right away, but thought better of it. It seemed best for Sam not to know where Riley and her colleagues were and what they were doing—at least not yet.

They had all stayed at the crime scene until the local cops had things fully under control. Even while they'd been wrapping things up there, Riley had kept worrying about the news of Art Kuehling's disappearance.

How long had he been missing tonight?

Was he gone at the time when Vanessa Pinker had been killed?

And what about when Gareth Ogden was murdered?

Did she have to consider Sam's father a suspect in the hammer murders?

Riley hadn't sensed anything hostile about the man. But Sam had said that he'd spent many years brooding about the Bonnett killings. Now that his mind was starting to go, could his obsession have taken a darker turn? Was he dementedly acting out the very violence that had haunted him all these years?

And if Art Kuehling *had* killed both of the recent victims, might he not even know it, at least not whenever he was safely inside the assisted living facility?

All of Riley's ruminations also led to the question of whether he'd been involved in that horrible family extermination ten years ago. Had he murdered the Bonnett family, or if not, might he have known all this time who had?

Riley, Jenn, and Bill got out of the car and walked into Hume Place. At the front desk, Riley asked to talk to someone about Art Kuehling. The receptionist paged Nurse Spahn, who arrived quickly.

Nurse Spahn looked startled to see the FBI agents.

"Hello again," she said. "What brings you here at this hour? Does this have something to do with Mr. Kuehling? Does anybody know where he is?"

Riley said, "Yes, I just got a text message from his daughter. She says she's found him."

Nurse Spahn sighed deeply and said, "Thank God!"

Then Riley said, "I need for you to tell me when he left the facility tonight."

Nurse Spann squinted and said, "I'm told that he checked himself out at eight o'clock. Why?"

This wasn't what Riley wanted to hear …

Vanessa Pinker was killed around nine fifteen.

Then Riley mentioned the date of Gareth Ogden's murder.

She asked the nurse, "Could you find out if he was missing that night—and if so, during what hours?"

"I think so," Nurse Spahn said.

She walked over to a nearby desk sat down at a computer and punched a few keys.

Then the nurse said, "Yes, as a matter of fact, he did slip out that night. Between seven and eleven."

Riley's heart sank at the realization …

We now have a suspect.

And that suspect was Sam's father.

CHAPTER THIRTY

Sam felt overwhelmed and confused by her own emotions as she sat down with her father and Tony at the table where they'd been working. Dominic plopped into a nearby chair, and she was grateful that her partner didn't seem to be in a hurry to leave.

On the one hand, Sam was deeply relieved to have found Dad safe and sound and in the company of an old friend like Tony. And of course, she was also angry that he'd caused her so much panic.

But she felt something else that was deep, strong, and troubling …

What is this feeling?

She quickly realized—it was sadness, pure and simple.

The fishing fly Dad had been working on when they came in was still gripped in the heavy black vise fastened to the edge of the table. A bunch of finished flies lay on the table. She'd watched Dad make countless hand-tied flies like these in his own workshop at home while she'd been growing up, and once again she admired his skill and craftsmanship.

Seeing him at work at this again brought back a lot of memories. She and her dad would gather up his latest flies in their tackle boxes, and he'd take her out fishing to the Gulf shore, the nearby river, and some of Mississippi's lovely lakes. Their favorite fishing was for large white trout right here in the area.

Right now he was happily showing her the batch of flies he'd been making since he'd arrived at Tony's house. He proudly waved one with a furry body and a yarn tail and clipped bits of feather. It was colored brown, olive, yellow, and black.

"Looky here, Punkin," he said to his daughter. "Do you remember me teaching you to make Woolly Worms like this when you were little?"

Sam nodded and almost said …

"I could never make them like you did."

But she felt as though she might cry if she said it aloud.

It had been a long time since she'd seen her father look so happy. As Dad continued showing her the completed flies, Sam glanced over at Dominic, asking him with a wordless, pleading expression ...

What should I say?

What should I do?

Dominic replied with a sad, silent shrug.

Meanwhile, her dad kept right on chattering about the fishing flies. Sam gently interrupted ...

"Dad, you can't do this anymore. I mean—you can't just go running off like this. You've ..."

She paused, wondering exactly what she was trying to stay.

Then she remembered something Nurse Spahn had told her yesterday ...

"If he goes out like that again—even once—I'm afraid we'll have to limit his activities ..."

Sam gulped hard as she thought ...

He blew his last chance.

She said slowly, "Dad, you've got to stay put. Right there in Hume Place. From now on."

Her father gave her an odd sort of smile.

Sitting across the table, Tony said, "Don't you think he knows that, kid? That's why he came over here. Just one last night hanging out with an old pal."

Her father added, "Punkin, you and I both talked to Nurse Spahn yesterday, so let's not mince words here. I'm losing what's left of my mind. I'm going to need a lot of extra care from here on in. They're going to shut me up with all the other folks who can't take care of themselves anymore, and before I know it I'll be wearing a diaper and they'll spoon feed me baby food. And I'm never getting out again. Not without a caretaker of some kind."

He gestured to the flies he'd been making and said ...

"And I'll never get to do *this* again."

As Sam looked at all the beautiful, feathery lures gathered together on the table, she was seized by a heartbreaking realization. Her father was also never likely to get to go fishing with the flies he'd been making tonight.

She couldn't control her emotions anymore.

She let out a sob and started crying.

Her father put a warm hand on her shoulder and said in a gentle voice ...

"Hey, don't be like that. I've had a good life. I've got no regrets. And I'm sorry I gave you such a scare. That was wrong of me."

Sam wiped her eyes and nose and tried to pull herself together.

She managed to choke out, "Dad, if you wanted to do this … hang out with Tony … why didn't you just tell me?"

Tony said, "Come on, kid. Would you have let him?"

Sam was surprised by the question.

"Of course I would," she said. "Why wouldn't I let him?"

Tony shrugged and added, "Well then, that kind of settles it, doesn't it? Let him spend the rest of the night here, and maybe part of tomorrow too. You can take him back to the old folks' joint tomorrow. I'll keep him out of trouble, I promise."

Sam looked back and forth at Tony at her father. She wondered—was there any reason not to let him do as he liked, at least tonight?

Her father added, "And don't let us run you off, Punkin. Hang around, set a spell, have a beer, make a couple of flies of your own. And you too, Dominic. Sam'll teach you how to make 'em, if you don't know already."

Sam almost smiled at the idea before she remembered …

The murder.

She had barely thought about it since she'd gotten here. It seemed that her dad and Tony had no idea what had happened. Unlike all the gawkers at the murder scene, Tony apparently wasn't linked to Rushville's gossip network.

She was about to explain that she and Dominic had to hurry back to work when her cell phone buzzed. She took the call and heard Agent Paige's voice.

"Sam, are you with your father?"

"Yes," Sam said, a bit surprised that Agent Paige would be concerned about her dad.

"Where is he?" Agent Paige said. "Where are you?"

"At the house of an old friend of his," Sam said.

"How long has he been there?" Agent Paige asked.

Sam quickly thought back to what Tony had told her when she'd first arrived.

"Since about eleven," she said. "Why?"

An unsettling silence fell.

Then Agent Paige said, "You texted me that you were bringing him back. I need for you to do that right away. Agents Roston and Jeffreys and I are already here—at Hume Place. We'll be waiting for you."

Agent Paige ended the call, and Sam sat staring at the phone.

Orders were orders, and she had to do as she was told.

Even so, she wondered …

What are the FBI agents doing at Hume Place?

*

Riley and her two FBI colleagues were standing inside the front doorway at Hume Place when she saw the cop car approaching. She could see that Sam was driving, and Dominic and her father were passengers.

Jenn murmured to Riley …

"Do you think it's possible? Do you think Art Kuehling really killed Gareth Ogden and Vanessa Pinker?"

Riley didn't reply.

The truth was, it seemed all too possible, at least at the moment. And he was the only possibility they'd turned up so far.

She hoped that the next few moments would prove her suspicions wrong.

She watched as Sam parked. Then Sam and the two others got out of the car and hurried into the building.

"What's the matter?" Sam asked Riley. "Is something wrong?"

Riley swallowed hard and said …

"Let's all sit down."

Riley and the five others found comfortable places to sit in the lobby. Before Riley spoke, she eyed Art Kuehling carefully. She asked herself—did he really look like a man who had brutally murdered a woman earlier that night?

He was dressed in cool summer clothes, and she didn't see a drop of blood anywhere on him. But Riley knew that was far from proof of innocence. Like Ogden's killing, Vanessa Pinker's murder had been clean, swift, and brutal. There had been plenty of blood around the woman's head, but most of it had surely been shed after she'd hit the ground.

The murderer might have escaped the scene with very little blood on him. It could have been easy enough to clean himself off quickly and completely. A change of clothes might not even have been necessary.

Art might well have done all this in a state of terrible mental confusion. At least he'd had opportunity. If he had actually killed two people, would he remember what he did, or why?

In a steady, quiet voice, Riley asked the man …

159

"Mr. Kuehling, do you know what time you left the facility tonight?"

Art wrinkled his brow and shook his head.

Bill said, "Nurse Spahn says you checked yourself out at eight o'clock."

Smiling weakly, Art said, "Well, I guess she'd know."

Riley fell silent for a moment, then said …

"Your daughter told me on the phone that you arrived at your friend's house at about eleven."

Art squinted as he said, "If she says so. I guess I'm not sure."

Riley gazed into his eyes. His expression was starting to seem foggy.

She said, "Art, could you please tell me where you went and what you were doing after you left here, and before you went to your friend's house?"

Art slowly shook his head.

"I … I really don't remember. I don't even remember checking out of here, really. I just remember … being at Tony's house and …"

Then he looked at his daughter and asked, "Me and Tony—we were making fishing flies, weren't we?"

Sam took hold of her father's hand and nodded, looking deeply concerned.

Riley took a long, slow breath.

Then she said, "Art, are you aware that a woman was murdered tonight?"

Art nodded slightly and said, "Why—yes. Sam told me about that just now, when we were driving here. But what does that have to do with …?"

His voice faded and he stared at Riley.

He's starting to get it, Riley thought.

Sam gasped aloud and said, "Agent Paige … surely you're not saying …"

Then Sam jumped to her feet with a wild expression.

She almost shouted, "No! This is crazy! How dare you even—"

To Riley's surprise, Art sharply interrupted her.

"Sam, stop it. Sit down. Let's talk about this."

Sam sat down next to her father, her face shaken and pale. He took hold of her hand again and spoke in a gentler and surprisingly lucid voice …

"Sam, I'm a cop, and you're a cop. We both understand the

nature of the job. Put yourself in Agent Paige's place. And her partners, too. How does this look to them? I can't account for my whereabouts when two murders took place. It's not just that I don't have an alibi. I don't have any idea where I was or what I was doing."

Tears were pouring down Sam's face.

She stammered, "But Dad, we both know you couldn't possibly …"

Art patted her on the shoulder and said, "Punkin, I didn't hurt anybody. I promise. And the sooner we clear this up, the better."

Then Art looked at Riley and her colleagues.

He said, "So are you going to arrest me? No need to read me my rights if you do. You won't need cuffs, I promise."

Riley shook her head and said, "Let's just go down to the police station. We'll talk there. And then we'll see …"

Art nodded, suddenly looking tired and old. Then he got to his feet and leaned on his daughter's shoulder. As the group went outside into the hot night air and walked toward the car, Art's words rattled through Riley's mind …

"Punkin, I didn't hurt anybody. I promise."

From his tone of voice, Riley doubted that he was entirely sure of that himself.

Riley glanced over at Bill and sensed that he was thinking what she was thinking …

We may have just found a serial killer.

It felt strange to hope so strongly that she was wrong.

CHAPTER THIRTY ONE

As Bill drove toward the police station, Riley took out her cell phone and punched in Chief Crane's number.

She wondered …

How am I going to explain this?

Riley was sitting in the back seat next to Art Kuehling, and Jenn was in the front passenger seat beside Bill. Sam and Dominic were following behind in their police car.

As she listened to the phone ringing, Riley studied Art's face. He was just staring at the street ahead with a glazed expression, as if he didn't know where he was or what was going on.

Riley wondered …

How on earth are we going to get any information out of him?

When Crane answered the phone, Riley asked, "Chief, are you at the station right now?"

"Yeah, I got back from the crime scene a little while ago. It's getting to be a hell of a long night. Why?"

Riley paused for a moment, then said …

"We're on our way to the station. We need to have the interrogation room ready."

She heard the chief let out a gasp.

"Jesus," he said. "Do you have a suspect in custody?"

Riley swallowed hard.

She couldn't bring herself to say the word "yes."

Instead she said, "Just get things ready."

As the two cars pulled up and stopped in front of the police station, Riley was relieved not to see a crowd of gawkers and reporters hanging around. Of course it was really late now, so public excitement had waned, and there really wasn't anything to see here anyway.

Instead, Riley saw a rotund man sitting alone on the front steps, smoking a cigar.

Amos Crites, she realized with dismay.

She'd spotted him in the crowd a while ago at the crime scene. He seemed to be following the case closely …

Maybe too closely, Riley thought. *Why would he be so*

interested?

Riley helped Art Kuehling out of the car and began to lead him by the arm toward the front door.

Riley heard Jenn let out a yelp of disgust as she and Dominic got out of their car.

"Crites," she demanded, "what the hell are you doing here?"

Crites sneered and shook some ashes off his cigar and stood up.

"Why, I'm here as a concerned citizen, of course," he said in a mock-sincere growl. "Just making myself available in case I can be of any help."

Then he chuckled harshly and added …

"And you folks sure could use some help, couldn't you? With another corpse on your hands and all. It's a shame, ain't it? This case seems to be too much for even the Feds to handle. Must be pretty embarrassing for y'all."

Then he glowered at Jenn's African-American features.

"I blame it on poor enlistment policies. The FBI's really scraping the bottom of the barrel these days."

Riley could see Jenn's face twist with anger.

She hastily reached out and touched Jenn lightly on the shoulder to caution her not to engage. The last thing they needed right now was a physical altercation between Jenn and the bigoted property owner.

Crites looked pleased to have provoked Jenn into reacting at all.

He said, "Well, as always, let me know if I can be of any service. For instance, maybe you want to know where I was and what I was doing when that woman was killed tonight."

Crites winked and added, "Don't worry about me, I can always come up with a good alibi."

Crites walked off the steps and continued on down the street.

Riley watched after him for a moment, wondering whether they were about to question the wrong man. Amos Crites had stirred her suspicions from the start. He'd had motive for killing Gareth Ogden, and for all they knew he also had opportunity.

As for a motive for killing Vanessa Pinker—well, having a serial killer at large in Rushville was sure to bring down property values, making it easier for Crites to buy up everything in sight. He didn't strike Riley as the kind of man who would have too many scruples about getting rid of a few people to fill his own pockets.

Of course Riley knew they had no cause to arrest Crites, and she regretted that they hadn't had the resources to keep a closer eye on him so far …

If I'm wrong about Art Kuehling, tracking Crites might have even saved another life.

But there was no point in thinking about that right now. She had to find out the truth about Kuehling. She escorted him through the glass doors, with the other cops and agents following behind.

Waiting inside was Chief Carter Crane. When he saw them, his mouth dropped open with shock.

Crane gasped, "*This* is your suspect? Art Kuehling? Christ, you've got to be kidding me."

There weren't many other cops in the station at this hour. The few who were present stood up from their desks at the sound of Crane's exclamation. They all looked as shocked as their chief did.

One barked, "What the hell do you guys think you're doing?"

"Art's one of us," another said.

One of the burlier cops took a menacing step toward Riley, growling, "Take your dirty Fed hands off our friend."

With tears in her eyes, Sam stepped between the cop and Riley.

She said sharply, "Back off, Carwell."

Then turning toward the other cops she added, "The same goes for the rest of you. Mind your own business. Don't make this harder than it already is."

Riley felt a surge of gratitude toward Sam. The young woman could easily have sided with her police colleagues to protest the arrest of her father. This whole incident was obviously terribly painful for her.

Shaking his head with disbelief, Carter Crane led the group to the interrogation room. Riley quickly decided to let Bill conduct the interview alone. As confused as he was, she guessed that Art Kuehling might think more clearly with only one person asking questions. Jenn had less experience, and Riley felt that she herself should stay at Sam's side and offer her comfort if it became necessary.

Riley, Sam, Dominic, and Jenn stood in the adjoining booth watching through the two-way mirror and listening over the intercom as Bill and Art Kuehling sat down at the table facing each other.

*

164

Sam fought back her tears as the interview got underway. She felt as though her heart would break.

Poor Dad.

After decades of loyal service, here he was being interrogated like a common criminal. She reminded herself that the FBI agents had good reason for questioning him—or at least it seemed so to them. And back at the assisted living facility, her father had been more than willing to cooperate.

But now he looked baffled and confused, as if he didn't know where he was, let alone what he was doing here. Sam realized that the shock of being brought here at such a strange hour must have suddenly worsened his mental condition.

Fortunately, Agent Jeffreys seemed intent on handling things with consideration, respect, and patience.

Jeffreys asked, "Mr. Kuehling, could you tell me why you're here?"

Sam's father squinted his eyes, seeming to think hard for a moment.

Finally he said, very slowly, "Yes, I think I remember. Something happened earlier tonight. Was someone killed? Yeah, it was like what happened to Gareth Ogden, wasn't it? Only it was a woman this time. And … and I can't account for my whereabouts when …" He hesitated again and then added, "When it happened."

Jeffreys nodded. Sam realized that the agent was gently trying to coax back her father's memory of what had taken place tonight.

Jeffreys said, "Do you know where the murder took place?"

Sam's father shook his head.

Jeffreys fell silent.

Sam wondered …

Why doesn't Agent Jeffreys say it was the movie theater parking lot?

But she quickly realized—the agent didn't want to lead Dad on in any way. In his present state, Dad might jump to conclusions—maybe even become convinced of his own guilt. It was best for Agent Jeffreys to tell him as little as possible, just help him think things through and remember on his own.

Jeffreys said, "Mr. Kuehling, do you remember leaving Hume Place earlier tonight?"

Dad shrugged and said in a docile tone, "I'm doing my best not to break the rules. They say if I don't behave, they'll have to put me in a different ward, keep me under closer watch, take away my privileges, treat me like a regular imbecile. I can't let that happen. I've got to cooperate."

"I understand how you feel," Jeffreys said. "And what are you doing to cooperate?"

Dad seemed to relax a little, as if this were only a casual conversation.

"Well, just follow the rules, of course," Dad said. "For example, when I went out tonight, I signed out properly and promised to be back at midnight."

"What time did you go out?" Jeffreys asked.

"Eight o'clock, I think," Dad said.

Sam breathed a little easier.

He's starting to remember.

Soon maybe he'd remember what had happened during those three lost hours, and the FBI agents would know once and for all that he wasn't a murderer.

Then Jeffreys said, "But according to the facility staff, you didn't come back at midnight."

Dad tilted his head.

"Didn't I? Hm, that doesn't sound very smart of me."

Then he chuckled a little and added, "Oh, yeah. I stopped in to visit my old buddy Tony Appleton. He was a cop like me, you know. Well, one thing led to another, and we started talking, and then we started making fishing flies—"

Jeffreys gently interrupted …

"Mr. Kuehling, you didn't go see your friend immediately after you left the facility."

Dad sat back in his chair.

"Didn't I? I'm sure I did. I remember it clearly."

Then with a growl of resentment he added, "I went to see Tony, and you and I both know it. You're just trying to confuse me."

Jeffreys shook his head and said, "I assure you, I'm not trying to confuse you. It's just a fact—after you left the facility, you were someplace else for three hours. Then you went to your friend's house. We need you to remember what you were during those three hours."

Sam's father suddenly slammed his fist on the table.

He almost shouted, "Why the hell are you asking me these questions? What did I do wrong?"

Sam was shaken by this outburst. She could barely remember her father ever losing his temper …

It's too much for him—all this pressure and suspicion.

Her father's face reddened, and his voice began to shake with rage …

"Do you have any idea what it's like, whoever the hell you are? Having your own brain turn against you, I mean? And not being able to trust anybody, not even the people closest to you? No, you don't know anything about it. Until you do, you'd better just leave me the hell alone."

Dad started to rise from his chair. Agent Jeffreys reached over and gently took hold of his wrist.

"Please stay seated, Mr. Kuehling," he said. "We need your help."

Dad scowled, but he sat back down. He leaned across the table, staring daggers at Agent Jeffreys.

"You need *my* help? That's a laugh! I'm the one who needs help, let me tell you! And is anybody going to help me? Fat chance of that."

Sam's breath was coming in gasps now.

What's happening to him? she wondered.

Her father waved around at the interrogation room and barked, "We're in the damned police station, aren't we? Well, why don't you go out in front and ask those guys there if any of them give a damn about me? Ask them the last time any of them visited me. They'll tell you never. And that'll be the truth."

The look on his face really frightened Sam.

Then he said, "Hell, nobody comes to visit me anymore. My own daughter has forgotten I'm even alive."

Sam felt as though she'd been stabbed in the heart.

That's not true, she thought.

She visited her father as often as she possibly could. But in his confused state right now, he couldn't seem to remember even that.

Then Dad said, "The last visitor I had at that stupid place was a goddamn mailman. Can you believe that?"

Sam's mouth dropped open.

Mailman!

She knew it meant something, although she couldn't yet bring what it was to mind.

Agent Jeffreys said, "The mailman?"

"Yeah," Dad growled. "The mailman who used to deliver at my house. He came to see me. Nobody else cares about me anymore. Nobody else remembers me."

Sam felt a tingling all over as she started to grasp the significance of what her father was saying.

She turned toward Agent Paige and said in an urgent voice …

"I've got to go in there. I've got to talk to my father. Right now."

CHAPTER THIRTY TWO

Sam waited anxiously for Agent Paige to reply. The FBI profiler was just staring back at her with an incredulous expression.

What if she says no? Sam wondered.

She just had to get into that interrogation room and talk to her father.

Sam was well aware that her request was irregular. How could a cop do a valid interview of her own parent? But she'd seen a hint of something that she needed to follow up on. And she didn't think anybody else could do it.

When no answer came, Sam repeated her request.

"Please, Agent Paige. Let me go in there."

Agent Paige said, "Sam, I know this is an upsetting experience for you, but—"

Sam interrupted, "If you just let me talk with him, I think you'll soon understand."

Agent Paige was quiet for a moment. Then, seeming to sense the urgency of Sam's plea, she nodded her reluctant approval. Before Sam went into the interrogation room, she looked at the other people in the booth—Dominic, Agent Roston, and Chief Crane.

She said to them, "Somebody please call Hume Place and have them check their visitor log. Find out if Wylie Pembroke visited my dad. If so, find out when it was."

Dominic's eyes widened with surprise, and Chief Crane's mouth dropped open.

Dominic replied, "But Wylie Pembroke …"

"Yeah, I know," Sam said. "But please just check."

Without another word, Sam hurried into the interrogation room. Agent Jeffreys looked startled to see her.

She said in a shaky, pleading voice, "Agent Jeffreys, just let me talk to him for a moment. Please."

Jeffreys hesitated and glanced toward the two-way mirror where he knew Riley was watching. When no protest came, he got up from his chair and stepped back from the table. Sam sat down in his place. She reached across the table and took her father's hands in hers. He smiled at the sight of her face.

"Punkin, I'm so glad to see you," he said.

"I'm glad to see you too, Dad," Sam said, struggling not to burst into tears. "Now listen. You just said a mailman came to visit you at Hume Place."

Dad nodded and said, "Yeah, Wylie Pembroke. You remember Wylie, don't you? He delivered our mail in the old days when you were growing up. Hell of a nice guy."

"Sure, I remember," Sam said.

And indeed, she remembered Mr. Pembroke really well—a kindly, smiling man, who seldom spoke. Folks said he had become mysteriously reclusive ever since his wife had left him. Back when he'd delivered their mail, Sam had often sensed something sad, haunted, and even regretful in his silence.

She asked her father, "Can you remember—when was it that he came by to see you at Hume Place?"

Her father's expression was changing now, as if some sort of a fog was lifting. The sight of Sam's face seemed to be bringing him back to his lucid self.

"It was a couple of weeks ago, I'm pretty sure," Dad said.

Sam inhaled sharply.

A couple of weeks!

She hoped that someone at Hume Place could confirm that visit.

The question was, why had such a silent, reclusive man gone to an assisted care facility to visit a retired cop—a cop he had rarely spoken to for years?

She squeezed her father's hands and said …

"Dad, do you remember what happened to Wylie soon after you saw him?"

He stared at her for a moment, then said …

"He killed himself. He hanged himself in his own home."

Sam nodded, and her father continued …

"He came to see me just the day before it happened. I was really shocked by the news when I heard about it. And Wylie was …"

Dad squinted in thought.

Then he said, "He was really troubled when he came to see me. He kept saying, 'Art, there's something I've got to tell you.' And, 'Art, there's something I've been keeping a secret for too long.' And, 'If I don't tell you now, I'm afraid I never will.' But he

170

wouldn't come out and say what he meant. Finally he just said goodbye and went away."

Sam asked, "How did he seem when he left?"

"He suddenly seemed—well, happy, even peaceful. Like he'd settled something in his own mind once and for all."

Sam's father scratched his chin.

"Then the next day, when I heard the news that he'd killed himself, I thought maybe he'd just wanted to tell me what he was going to do, but couldn't bring himself to say it. I felt guilty, because I thought maybe I should have guessed what was wrong and said something to stop him. And I couldn't understand why he'd want to talk to *me* about it. But now …"

Dad's voice faded for a moment.

Sam could tell by his eyes that he was coming to the same conclusion as she had.

"My land," he murmured. "Wylie came to see me … because he wanted to confess."

Sam inhaled sharply as he confirmed her thoughts.

She reminded herself …

Keep coaxing him.

Let him think it through himself.

He needs this.

She asked, "What did he want to confess to?"

Her father's eyes were bright and alert now. He seemed like his old keen self again.

He gasped aloud and said, "He wanted to tell me he'd killed the Bonnetts."

"Why do you think he wanted to tell *you*?" Sam asked.

Dad said, "Because he knew—everyone in town knew—that case has been eating me up inside for years. I've felt worse about it than anybody else—about not solving it in all this time. And he wanted to put my mind at ease at long last, and his own mind as well. But when he tried to say it, he just couldn't. Instead, right there and then he thought of another way to deal with his pain and guilt. He'd kill himself. That's why he seemed so peaceful when he left."

Sam could hardly contain her joy and relief.

She said, "Dad, we just solved it. We finally solved the Bonnett murders. You and me together."

Her father smiled broadly and said …

"We did at that, didn't we, Punkin?"

Then Sam looked around at Agent Jeffreys, who was standing back from the table. She could tell by his smile and his twinkling eyes that he was both pleased and impressed by what he had just witnessed.

Sam, followed by Jeffreys, rushed out of the interrogation room into the adjoining booth. When she saw the eager and surprised faces of Chief Crane, Dominic, and the two female FBI agents, she exclaimed …

"Did you hear that? Did you hear what just happened?"

Chief Crane said, "I sure as hell did. Jesus, what a discovery."

Dominic said to her, "While you were in there, I called Hume Place, and they checked the guest log. Your dad's right. Wylie Pembroke did come to visit with him the day before he killed himself."

Agent Paige looked especially excited. She said to Chief Crane …

"Now we need evidence. And I think we both know where we need to look for it."

Crane nodded and said, "Let's go."

CHAPTER THIRTY THREE

As she looked out into the earliest light of morning, Riley's mind was flooded with confusion. She was crowded into the back seat of the FBI car with Jenn and Sam's partner, Dominic Wolfe. Bill was driving, and Chief Crane sat beside him in the passenger seat giving directions. Sam wasn't with them—she'd rushed off in the other car to follow a different lead. The young cop had been excited over a call from Brandon Hitt saying he thought he could clear her father, so Riley let her go meet him.

Riley and the rest of the team were headed for the apartment where the mailman, Wylie Pembroke, had killed himself. It seemed highly possible that they were about to solve the Bonnett family murders once and for all. If so, Riley knew she ought to feel happy for both Sam and her father. At long last, and with Sam's help, Art Kuehling had achieved the redemption he had sought all these years …

And yet …

She knew that the mailman Wylie Pembroke had killed himself two weeks ago. He'd been dead since shortly before Gareth Ogden's murder. He had definitely not killed either Ogden or Vanessa Pinker.

Riley shuddered a little as she thought …

That still leaves Art Kuehling as a possible suspect.

Art had silently acknowledged as much before they'd left the police station just now. He hadn't asked to be taken back to Hume Place. Instead, he'd politely asked to be put into a cell so he could rest from the night's terrible ordeal.

Riley wished with all her heart she could clear him. But she remembered how angry he'd gotten with Bill during the questioning, slamming his fist on the table and almost yelling …

"Why the hell are you asking me these questions? What did I do wrong?"

It had been shocking behavior from a man who had seemed so gentle just moments before. But did it suggest that Art was capable of murder? It was surely just as likely that his rising dementia was all that had provoked his outburst.

And then, of course, there was Amos Crites, lurking about like

173

some sort of buzzard in search of dead flesh. Wasn't he at least as likely a suspect as Art Kuehling? Riley wished she'd had just cause to bring Crites in for questioning. And she couldn't help hoping that the wrong man was now sleeping in that jail cell.

They drove far away from the beach into the neighborhood where Wylie Pembroke had lived—a row of tan-colored apartment buildings that all looked exactly alike. Of course the local police had been over Pembroke's apartment after the suicide, but they were just checking to be sure there were no signs of it being a homicide. Because the mailman had left no surviving family, and nobody had made any claims to his things, Chief Crane still had the key. They didn't even need a warrant to search the place again.

Bill parked, and they got out of the car and headed toward a ground-floor apartment. Chief Crane unlocked the door and they went inside.

Like the exterior of the building, the smallish apartment seemed uncannily neat and disagreeably bland inside. The furniture was basic and functional. If Riley didn't already know that Wylie had owned this place, she'd have guessed that it was a pre-furnished rental apartment. It was hard to imagine anyone deliberately surrounding himself with this kind of impersonal generic furniture.

On the way over, Chief Crane had mentioned that Wylie's wife had left him about a decade ago and moved far way—to Minneapolis, Crane thought. Nobody knew why the marriage had fallen apart. It seemed pretty obvious to Riley that Wylie had moved into this place after the breakup.

She glanced around and saw some pictures hanging on the walls. None of them were Wylie Pembroke's wife. Instead, they showed a young boy, smiling proudly as he held fish that he seemed to have caught. The boy was younger in some pictures, older in others. So Riley knew that the photos had been taken during the course of several years.

Riley turned to Chief Crane and said …

"Show me where Wylie Pembroke killed himself."

Chief Crane led the group over to a bedroom doorway. He had a folder full of grim photos of the suicide scene and showed them to Riley and Bill, explaining what had happened …

"Pembroke hanged himself off this open door. He tied a noose in one end of a length of rope, and he tied the other end to this doorknob. He threw the noose over the door, climbed up onto a chair, and put his head into the noose. Then he kicked the chair out from under him."

Chief Crane went on to tell Riley and Bill that Pembroke's cleaning lady had found him the next morning, and he explained how he and his team had made sure that there was no evidence of foul play.

Riley trembled at an unwelcome memory—the image of a woman hanging by her neck from a cord tied to an ornate light fixture …

Marie Sayles.

A little over a year ago, Riley's friend Marie had hanged herself. She took her own life out of despair upon realizing that a psychopath who had once tormented both her and Riley was stalking her again.

Riley could remember her frantic phone conversation with Marie as she drove to her apartment, hoping to arrive in time to save her.

"There's nothing you can do," Marie had said. *"You're not going to do anything. Nobody's going to do anything. Nobody can do anything."*

Marie had said those words just before kicking a stepladder out from under herself and strangling to death.

Riley had spent months trying to put that horrible episode behind her. But the pictures of Wylie Pembroke's dead body brought the memory back, and she found herself once again fighting back her guilt and grief.

Not now, she reminded herself sternly. *You've got work to do.*

Riley quickly pulled herself together. She told herself that Pembroke's suicide was not at all like Marie's. It was clear to her that he hadn't killed himself out of fear or desperation. He'd done so coolly and deliberately, perhaps even with relief.

She remembered what Art Kuehling had said a little while ago …

"He suddenly seemed—well, happy, even peaceful. Like he'd settled something in his own mind once and for all."

Riley felt more and more sure that Sam and her father were right—Pembroke had killed the Bonnett family and had spent ten long years struggling with guilt and horror at his deed.

He'd finally put an end to that guilt and horror by killing himself …

And yet …

They still didn't have hard evidence to prove that scenario.

Riley's thoughts were interrupted by the sound of her cell phone buzzing. She took the phone out of her pocket and saw that she'd received a text message from Sam ...

On my way to the fishing pier. Hope to find Brandon there.

Riley suppressed a sigh of annoyance. When Sam had left on her own, she'd told Riley that she was looking for Brandon, apparently thinking he could provide an alibi for her dad during the recent murders. Sam had said she expected to meet him in the diner. That didn't seem to have worked out. The young cop had been understandably eager to find out about that. But while it was good of Sam to report where she was, it hardly mattered to Riley at the moment.

Riley told Chief Crane that she wanted to explore the rest of the apartment. She and her three companions went on into the small, nondescript kitchen, which had been kept as neat as the rest of the house. She opened up a closet and found a pegboard with a complete set of hand tools.

She felt a sudden chill as her eyes lighted on an ordinary claw hammer.

The head and the handle were encrusted with something dark.

She heard Jenn gasp and say ...

"Riley, do you think ... ?"

Riley didn't reply. She put on a pair of plastic gloves that she always kept with her. Then she reached out to the hammer and touched it and ...

"Oh my God," she murmured.

She felt the same charge of hatred she'd sensed at the Bonnett's abandoned home—the cold fury of the man who had killed the family. Her hands trembled a little as she took hold of the hammer and examined it more closely.

Sure enough, the encrusting substance was dried blood.

Riley said to her companions, "This is it. This is proof. I'm sure the DNA will match the Bonnett family."

Looking at the hammer with amazement, Bill added, "He never cleaned it during all those years. He must have left it like this as a reminder, to punish himself."

As Riley held the hammer, that feeling of fury faded. In its place she sensed shame and self-loathing. She knew that Bill was right. Wylie Pembroke had probably held this hammer every single day to remind himself of what he had done, to assure himself that it hadn't been just some nightmare ...

But he couldn't punish himself enough.

In the end, suicide had proved to be his only way out.

Chief Crane said, "I still don't understand. Wylie always seemed like such a nice guy. Nobody would have ever thought he was capable of murder."

Thinking again of the fury she'd felt at the Bonnett home, Riley said ...

"It was a crime of passion. It wasn't something he would normally even dream of doing. And after he did it, he had trouble believing he had done it. He was driven to do it by something really dire."

"But what?" Chief Crane asked.

What indeed? Riley thought.

She sensed that the answer to that question was somewhere right here in front of her. She looked closely at the closet walls but saw nothing odd. Then she stooped down and groped around the floor.

There!

She'd found a loose board.

Riley heart raced as she pulled the board away.

Under it was a shoebox. She opened it and saw that the old cardboard box was full of handwritten letters.

She unfolded one and saw ...

Dearest Connie—

I don't know how much longer I can keep going on like this. I love you so much and want you for myself ...

She glanced to the end of the letter and saw that it was signed ...

I love you always,
Cosmo

Chief Crane exhaled sharply as he looked at the letter over Riley's shoulder.

He said, "Cosmo Bonnett wrote these letters to Connie, Wylie's wife! They were having an affair!"

Riley nodded and said, "Wylie must have found these letters.

That's what drove him to murder. He was so wild with fury, it wasn't enough for him to just kill Cosmo. He killed the entire family."

"Is that even possible?" Crane asked. "Do people really do such things?"

Bill said, "We've seen things like this before. It really was a case of temporary insanity."

Crane slouched with discouragement and said, "We should have kept searching through the house after he killed himself. We should have found this."

Bill commented, "Why would you? As far as you knew, you were looking into a suicide. You had no reason to believe Wylie Pembroke was also a murderer."

Crane took the box and glanced through the letters. He still looked as if he could hardly believe his eyes.

Meanwhile, a vague tingle came over Riley—a feeling that they were still overlooking something vitally important.

Then she remembered …

Those pictures in the living room.

She said to Crane, "Didn't you tell me that Wylie didn't leave any surviving family?"

"That's right," Crane said.

Riley added, "And you said that he became reclusive after his wife left him."

"Yeah, a complete loner," Crane said. "He just kept delivering the mail. He was nice to everybody, but he didn't socialize, had no friends that anybody knew of. But good God—do you think Connie left him because she knew what he'd done?"

Possibly, Riley thought, without saying so aloud.

But Wylie's ex-wife wasn't what worried her at the moment.

Riley rushed back into the living room, followed by the others. She pointed to the pictures on the wall of the young boy holding the fish he'd caught.

She asked Crane, "If Wylie was such a recluse, who was the boy in these photos?"

Crane peered closely at the photos and said …

"Why, I recognize that kid. That's Brandon Hitt. He must have had some special relationship with Wylie. I never knew about it. I don't think anybody else did either."

Riley felt a jolt at those words …

A special relationship!

An impressionable young boy had become close to a man who harbored a terrible secret.

How might the boy have been shaped by that strange friendship?

What had he come to learn about his older friend?

And now that he was a grown man, how might he have reacted upon learning of Wylie's suicide?

Riley felt overwhelmed by questions she couldn't yet answer.

She was also seized by an awful thought …

Sam said she's on her way to meet Brandon.

Without a word to her companions, Riley grabbed her phone. She found Sam's number and punched it in. She could hear the phone ringing again and again and again.

She's not answering, Riley thought with dread.

CHAPTER THIRTY FOUR

As Sam walked out of the diner, she punched in a text message to Agent Paige …

On my way to the fishing pier. Hope to find Brandon there.

She didn't know whether it was important to keep Agent Paige informed of her whereabouts. But it seemed like the right thing to do, since Agent Paige had been kind enough to allow Sam to go look for Brandon in hopes of clearing her father.

She remembered her phone call from Brandon. He'd just called to check in on her, he'd said, which had seemed kind of him. But when she'd mentioned that her father was a suspect, he'd sounded alarmed …

"That's impossible, Sam. Your dad couldn't *have committed those murders. In fact I know …"*

But he'd balked at telling her …

"I'm sorry, it's nothing. I … misspoke."

He hadn't even told her where he was at the moment. But she'd heard restaurant noises in the background during the call—clattering dishes and servers taking orders. She knew that the all-night diner was the only eating establishment in Rushville that was open at this hour.

When Sam hadn't found Brandon in the diner, she'd asked a waitress where he might be.

The waitress had said …

"Oh, Brandon's always here in the early mornings. When he leaves, he says he's on his way down to the fishing pier. I guess he likes to go there and see the first sunlight on the water."

Sam wondered—was that where he had gone this time?

The fishing pier sounded like the best guess if she was going to catch up with Brandon. She really had to find out what he knew.

As she got into the car and started driving, she thought about the strange words Brandon had said to her over the phone …

"Your dad couldn't *have committed those murders."*

But then he'd said …

"I'm sorry, it's nothing. I ... misspoke."

What on earth did he know?

And why wouldn't he tell me?

Sam drove to the road that followed the waterfront and continued along it until she arrived at the fishing pier. The big old wooden structure jutted out about a hundred yards or so over the Gulf. She parked her car and got out.

When she first looked down at the beach, she had trouble seeing anything clearly in the pale early morning light, but her eyes quickly adjusted to the dimness. And sure enough, she could see a man standing alongside the pier, looking out over the waves that came roaring in with the rising tide.

She trotted down the beach, calling out …

"Brandon! Is that you?"

But he didn't seem to hear her over the sound of the surf.

Finally she walked up right behind him and said his name.

He turned around and gave her a big smile. It was Brandon, all right.

He said, "I've been expecting you."

Sam felt a flash of confusion.

Expecting me?

Why had he even supposed that she was coming here?

Suddenly he raised his right arm, and she saw a flash of metal in the faint light. She reflexively flinched as the hammer struck at her forehead. She felt a stab of pain, and her vision was filled with stars.

For a moment Sam barely knew where she was.

Then she heard her cell phone ringing.

In her confusion, she almost reached to answer it, but quickly realized …

Not now.

Sam struggled to come to her senses. She knew that this was a matter of life or death.

She vaguely realized that her flinch had been just enough to prevent him from striking a clean, deadly blow directly to her forehead.

She knew she had to overcome the pain. Another strike would come at any second.

And he'd make sure that it would kill her.

Lurching about clumsily, Sam felt water surging around her legs. She realized that she was wading out alongside the pier, and

181

that there was no escape in this direction.

When she turned around to find her way back to the beach, she saw Brandon wading toward her. Without stopping to think, Sam reached for the service revolver in her hip holster. Hastily, she yanked out the gun and fired a single desperate, poorly aimed shot.

She heard him grunt with pain and saw him whirl around and almost tumble into the waves.

She'd been lucky enough to graze him. Now she took more careful aim at his torso and pulled the trigger again.

Sam's gun jammed.

Brandon was stunned and staggering now, but she knew he wasn't badly injured. It wasn't enough to stop him from trying to kill her. Like a wounded animal, he was more dangerous than ever.

She wished she could run up the beach toward the car, but she knew she'd never make it past him.

She turned around and looked at the relentless waves.

There was only one avenue of escape—and that was among the pilings under the pier.

She holstered her useless weapon and pushed on into the pounding surf.

*

In a daze, Brandon gripped his wounded shoulder …
Such amazing pain.

He was sure it wasn't a serious wound. The bullet seemed to have passed straight through soft flesh and exited without hitting any bone.

Even so, he couldn't remember feeling such searing pain since …

When?

It hadn't been since he was a boy and his father had wreaked such terrible drunken punishment upon him.

For a moment he couldn't remember where he was or what he'd come here to do …

The woman.
Sam.

He'd targeted her for death when she'd come to his house with her partner and the FBI agents a couple of days ago—a random choice, just like the others.

He'd intended her to be his next victim after Vanessa Pinker.

Until just a moment ago, his plan was going perfectly. She was a smart young woman—too smart for her own good, just as he'd hoped. When he'd called her from the diner, he'd known she would hear the clatter of restaurant noise and realize where he was and come there at once. He also knew that one of the waitresses would tell her that he always came here.

The trick had been to make it seem like her own idea to follow him here.

And it had been a good trick—until the very moment he tried to strike.

Sam wasn't like Ogden or Vanessa. Her reflexes were swift and natural, and he hadn't been able to land the perfect blow he'd hoped for. He was disappointed in himself, but he knew that he didn't have time to wallow in frustration. He had to finish this. He had to strike again, and he had to make the next blow count.

But where was she right now?

He turned around and looked up and down the beach. He knew that he'd be able to see her if she'd fled up onto the sand.

Then he turned around and looked beneath the pier.

She's under there somewhere, he realized.

She must be crouched behind one of those big wooden pilings not far away.

He felt pleased again.

Now all he had to do was wade under the pier and search from piling to piling.

But as he plunged ahead into the water, breaking waves hit him with startling force. His thoughts were becoming jumbled due to blood loss and the shock of pain.

With unexpected power, memories slammed into Brandon's awareness.

It was as though he could see the kindly mailman he'd first gotten to know on his paper route when he was still a teenager. People had said Wylie Pembroke was a mysterious loner who had no friends, but he had befriended Brandon, making him feel special and wanted.

Images of long hours spent in in the man's little home raced through Brandon's mind. He remembered how they'd gone camping and fishing together.

They'd been fishing for trout one day when the man broke down and cried …

"I killed them, son. I killed them all. Nobody knows except

you."

Brandon had been astonished by this revelation—that his good-hearted friend was none other than the murderer of the entire Bonnett family …

The struggle against the waves brought Brandon back to the present. He was wading among the pilings now, still gripping his hammer tightly. He could see no sign of the young woman he intended to kill.

She had to be right there somewhere. But when he tried to focus on his search, he felt sick and dizzy and in pain, and memories kept distracting him.

He remembered how tormented the poor man had been by what he'd done.

That had always seemed unfair and unjust to Brandon.

After all, he had acted to right a wrong.

Cosmo Bonnett had had an affair with Wylie Pembroke's wife.

Wylie had a right to his revenge.

And what a breathtaking act of revenge it was—to take out Cosmo's family before finally killing the adulterer himself!

Waves were coming at Brandon harder and higher now, and he found it hard to stay on his feet, and he couldn't find his prey, and he still kept thinking about Wylie …

Brandon had always wished he had Wylie's courage and audacity. If he had, maybe he wouldn't have let his father cause so much grief to his mom and his little brother. He wouldn't have allowed his father to pound on his own young hands with a hammer, causing pain that still felt today and would surely suffer from for the rest of his life.

Maybe Brandon would have taken that hammer to his own father sometime when he lay sleeping, rather than let him run away from his abused family for good.

Brandon had spent years wishing he could be more like Wylie Pembroke. He wanted to be that brave, that powerful.

Whenever Brandon fantasized about doing what Wylie had done, he always imagined making one single improvement.

Wylie's act had been crazed and chaotic.

The whole town had buzzed with wild descriptions of the blood-drenched bedrooms and the crushed skulls and the pulverized, unrecognizable faces.

Brandon thought that the murder hadn't really been in keeping with his friend's character. Wylie's vengeance would have been better served by more coldness, calculation, swiftness, precision …

Neatness.

Brandon always dreamed of performing such an act to sheer perfection.

And then, two weeks ago, Wylie's guilt had caught up with him and he'd killed himself …

A wave broke high and strong and almost knocked Brandon down. The rising tide was slowing his search, but it brought him back to his present problem.

Did she get away? he wondered.

No, he couldn't imagine how she could have gotten past him. She still had to be somewhere near here, cringing behind a piling, hoping he'd give up his search and go away.

He wasn't going to do that.

I've got to do this—for Wylie.

For what were these murders except a tribute, a homage to a man Brandon had loved and respected despite that man's own guilt and self-loathing?

He'd hoped that Wylie was watching when he'd killed the man and the woman.

He'd hoped that Wylie's spirit could at last see that revenge been right all along.

He'd hoped he could show Wylie how beautiful such a deed could be.

But now it was all at risk, and things had gone awry. He had to finish this killing as best he could. It wouldn't be perfect, but …

There will always be time for another. It will be perfect next time.

Brandon's eye was caught by something bobbing behind one of the pilings.

She's there, he thought.

Another wave crashed past him as he approached the piling. He reached down under the water and groped around and felt a pair of hands pushing back at him vainly and frantically.

In another instant, he gripped her by the hair and pulled her face to the surface.

She gasped and coughed, still trying to push him away.

But he had a firm grip on her with his left hand, and his hammer was tightly gripped in his right, and now, with one single swift movement, he could …

Suddenly Brandon felt something close around his neck and

yank him backward. He found himself thrashing wildly, like one of those fish he and Wylie had caught when he was younger.

He felt himself pressing tightly against something enormous and soft.

Was it some sort of huge aquatic animal?

No, he realized. *It's a man.*

With a cry of fury, Brandon wrenched around to kill the intruder.

CHAPTER THIRTY FIVE

Jenn was the first one out of the FBI car when Bill pulled it to a stop on the waterfront drive in sight of the pier. She looked toward the big structure and saw a person staggering out of the surf and up onto the shore.

It's Sam! she realized.

Sam was drenched and appeared to be disoriented. Jenn saw that her head was bleeding near the temple. Jenn started running toward Sam, calling out her name.

Sam seemed to hear. She stared at Jenn dazedly and then pointed under the pier.

Jenn could see some kind of struggle going on in the water among the pilings.

What on earth?

In the shadowy morning light, she was able to make out two men fighting—one of them slim and tall, the other huge and bulky. Whatever was going on, Jenn knew that she had to stop it.

She plunged into the water and struggled through breaking waves. When she reached the combatants, Jenn saw that one of them was Brandon Hitt. He was holding a hammer in one hand and pushing someone's head underwater with the other. Two fat hands were pushing back at him.

Before Brandon could notice she was there, Jenn found her balance and threw a swift punch at his face. Her blow sent him reeling back into an oncoming wave.

Jenn grabbed at the figure submerged in the water, worrying that whoever it was had drowned already. But Brandon quickly recovered his footing, and raised his hammer to come after her again. His snarling expression revealed his intention to kill.

Just then a gunshot rang out.

A familiar voice yelled, "Freeze right there, Brandon Hitt, or the next one won't be into the air."

She turned and saw Agent Paige standing in the water's edge, her revolver pointed directly at Brandon. And she wasn't alone. Bill, Chief Crane, and Dominic were all thigh-deep in the surf, pointing their weapons at Brandon.

"They won't miss," Jenn warned her opponent.

Brandon dropped the hammer and raised his hands, looking defeated and exhausted.

Jenn reached again for the bulky human shape that was still submerged.

She grabbed hold of a shirt and pulled a face to the surface.

The man scrambled to get his footing, clinging to a piling and coughing so hard he seemed about ready to vomit.

Jenn recognized him at once.

She said, "Why, Amos Crites—as I live and breathe! What the hell are you doing here?"

Crites managed to say, "I'm doing your job, it seems to me."

His voice broke down in a fit of coughing.

"Come on," Jenn said, helping him struggle back onto the shore. She saw that Riley and Chief Crane were putting Brandon into handcuffs. Bill had gotten Sam wrapped up in a blanket he must have gotten from the car, and he was talking on his cell phone—calling an ambulance, Jenn was sure.

Crites grumbled, "I've been following you Feds around all night, ever since poor Vanessa Pinker got killed, watching you bumbling around getting nowhere. I got worried about Sam Kuehling once she took off on her own, and I started trailing her, and when I saw what kind of trouble she was in down here …"

Gasping for breath as she supported Crites's enormous bulk, Jenn pointed at Sam and said …

"Well, it looks like you saved Sam's life. Thanks for that. And I saved yours. You're welcome. And you might want to thank the Feds for scraping the bottom of the barrel for the likes of me."

Crites's coughing faded and he stared at her.

He finally seemed to register that he'd been saved by a black female FBI agent.

Crites shook his head and growled as he collapsed onto the sand.

Jenn couldn't help but laugh as she thought …

God sure does love irony.

CHAPTER THIRTY SIX

As Sam started to wake up, she realized that she was aching all over. Her head was splitting with pain.

Where am I? she wondered.

She opened her eyes, and her surroundings started to come into focus …

Oh, yeah. The hospital.

She'd been in and out of consciousness since her ordeal at the pier. She remembered being brought to the emergency room, where her head wound had been stitched and bandaged, and a doctor had run tests to make sure her concussion wasn't serious.

She noticed that some people were standing at one side of her bed. They were Agents Paige, Jeffreys, and Roston. Then she realized that someone on the other side of the bed was holding her hand. She turned her head slightly and saw her father smiling down at her. He looked like his old lucid self.

"Dad!" she said, surprised by the weakness in her voice.

Her father nodded and said, "That's right. They sprung me from jail as soon as they found out who the real killer is. And you're the one who led the Feds to him. I'm proud of you, Punkin."

Sam sighed, remembering how she'd allowed herself to get drawn into Brandon's trap. It didn't feel like anything to be proud of.

She said, "All I did was get myself into trouble."

Agent Paige spoke up. "I wouldn't say that. You and your father solved the Bonnett killings. That's quite an accomplishment all by itself."

Sam felt a glow come over her. The praise, especially from that particular agent, sounded sweet to her ears.

Then Agent Paige said, "Agents Jeffreys and Roston and I are headed back to Quantico. We just stopped by to check in on you before we left."

"That's nice of you," Sam said. "But what about Brandon?"

Agent Jeffreys said, "He's in another hospital room, getting his shoulder wound taken care of. Chief Crane is with him, and he's under heavy guard. He's been drugged up for his pain, and he's talking like crazy."

Sam said, "But why did he do it? Kill those people, I mean?"

Agent Roston said, "It's a long story. But when he was a young teenager, he seems to have developed some kind of a close relationship with the original killer, Wylie Pembroke. And he found out what Pembroke had done. After Pembroke killed himself, Brandon made some kind of warped decision to carry on his work."

Sam lay staring at the agents, trying to make sense of what she'd just heard.

Agent Paige said, "Don't worry, we'll know the whole truth pretty soon. Not that we'll ever entirely understand why he did what he did. In our line of work, we get used to dealing with things we can never fully understand."

Then someone else came through the door. It was Amos Crites.

"I see you're looking better," Crites said in his rumbling voice.

Sam remembered glimpsing Crites grabbing hold of Brandon just as he was ready to land a fatal blow of his hammer.

"Thanks for what you did for me," she said.

"It was nothing," Crites said with a shrug. "I should have figured out something was wrong with Brandon Hitt long ago. I've known him and his family from way back. One day when he was a kid, Brandon told me his dad was hitting him with a hammer, and I threatened the old man so bad that he left town for good."

Crites shuffled his feet and continued …

"I guess I was the only one in town who noticed how Brandon got close to Wylie Pembroke. I thought it was a good thing for both of them."

With a low growl, Crites added, "Boy, was I ever wrong."

Then he drew himself up again and said, "Anyway, this whole nasty thing is over with, and I'm damn glad of it. Folks just can't go around killing people for no good reason. It would've gotten bad for business before long."

Crites pulled out a cigar and almost lit it. Then he seemed to remember where he was, and he put the cigar back in his pocket.

"Don't get me wrong," he said. "I like it when property values drop, but only temporary-like, so I can buy up cheap. A few more murders and things might have gone sour around here permanently. I wouldn't like that."

As he turned to go, he found himself facing Agent Roston.

He scowled sharply at her, and she broke into laughter.

What's that all about? Sam wondered.

Without another word, Amos Crites left the room.

"We're going now too," Agent Paige said, patting Sam on the shoulder. "You're a talented young woman. You might have a future in our line of work. I'd like to stay in touch."

Barely able to believe her ears, Sam managed to gasp out a thank-you.

When the agents left, Sam saw that her father had fallen asleep in his chair.

Poor Dad, she thought.

What a terrible night he'd been through. And when he woke up, would he have any idea what had happened? Sam felt sick at heart as she thought about how his condition was going to worsen for the rest of his life. But she was also determined to spend as much time as she could with him from now on.

Sam was almost ready to drop off to sleep herself when Dominic arrived with a bouquet of flowers.

"Hey," Dominic said quietly, trying not to awaken her father. "It's nice to see you looking better."

Dominic suddenly seemed more attractive than she'd ever noticed him to be before.

"You don't look so bad yourself," she said.

Then she felt herself blush …

Oh my God. Did I say that aloud?

Anyway, it was certainly true. She'd sensed for some time that Dominic had a thing for her, and his jealousy toward Brandon had pretty much proved it. And now she was surprised at how glad she was to see him.

Dominic sat down beside the bed and said, "The doctors say they'll be keeping you here for a couple of days, just for observation. That means I get to spend some quality time with you."

She took Dominic's hand and squeezed it.

"That sounds nice," she said.

She thought with a smile …

Maybe I had to get smacked with a hammer to find out how I feel about him.

CHAPTER THIRTY SEVEN

As the FBI plane landed at the Quantico airfield, Riley found herself thinking about her flight down to Mississippi just yesterday. So much had happened since then, she'd had no time to consider the dream she'd had during that trip.

In that dream, her father had told her …

"You can be right *about something, and* wrong *about it too, both at the same time.*

"Absolutely right, absolutely wrong."

Riley sighed at the memory. Now she knew how true those words had been. She'd sensed from the start that there was some deep connection between the murders of the Bonnett family and the killings of Gareth Ogden and Vanessa Pinker.

Her feelings at the crime scenes had confirmed that feeling— that the new murder was some kind of *continuation* …

She shivered a little as she remembered what her father had said …

"'A continuation.' An interesting choice of words."

She'd been convinced that the new killings weren't the work of some mere copycat, and that had turned out to be both true and not true.

By his own account, Brandon Hitt hadn't been trying to duplicate Wylie Pembroke's horrid crime of passion.

He'd been trying to improve upon it.

He'd been trying to perfect it.

Chief Crane had called her during the flight to tell her that he'd managed to get in touch with Wylie Pembroke's ex-wife, who was now living in Minneapolis. Crane said the poor woman had become hysterical when he told her all that had happened. Back when the Bonnett family had been killed, she'd suspected that her husband had taken his hideous revenge for her affair with Cosmo Bonnett. Feeling both fearful and guilty, she'd fled Rushville never to return.

But in the end, she hadn't been able to escape her past.

Riley wondered about Wyatt Hitt. It was no fault of his own that his father had left, his mother had died, and his brother turned out to be a cold and calculating killer. What chance did that young paperboy have to escape his past?

Fortunately, Wyatt wouldn't be left to foster care. Chief Crane had said that Amos Crites was taking responsibility for the boy's future. Crites had spurred a local church group into action and a good solid family was taking Wyatt in. Maybe the boy would be able to overcome his awful start in life.

Riley knew that it wouldn't be easy for Wyatt. After all, Jilly was still affected by terrible things that she'd been through and Riley would hardly describe her own early life as stable and solid.

Then Riley smiled and relaxed a little. In spite of Riley's frequent absences, Jilly was maturing fast and learning to deal with her occasional lapses into self-doubt. And of course Gabriela was a rock-solid influence. And Riley and Blaine could be on their way to … well, maybe a good solid family of their own.

The plane taxied to a stop, and Riley, Bill, and Jenn headed for the exit. As they stepped out of the plane, they saw Special Agent Brent Meredith standing below on the tarmac, his arms crossed and with a frown on his face.

Bill murmured to Riley as they went down the steps …

"I don't guess he's here to congratulate us on a job well done."

"No, I don't suppose he is," Riley said with a sigh.

She remembered the team chief's fury on the phone upon learning that she'd gone AWOL, and that Bill and Jenn had covered for her …

"There's going to be hell to pay for all three of you when you get back."

When they got to the bottom of the stairs, Meredith growled at Riley …

"I want a word with you."

Then he said to Bill and Jenn …

"I'll talk to you two later."

Bill and Jenn gave Riley sympathetic and worried looks and continued on their way.

Meredith said to Riley, "Is your car here?"

"Yes," Riley said.

"I'll walk you to it," Meredith said.

They walked in silence for a few tense moments.

Then Meredith said, "Tell me why you came back in the middle of a case."

Riley realized there was nothing to tell him but the truth. She explained as simply as she could that she'd found out that her younger daughter had been cutting herself, and she'd thought she needed to get back to her.

"How is your daughter now?" Meredith asked.

Riley was surprised by the question.

She said, "OK, the last time I saw her. She'd going to need counseling, though."

Another silence fell as they walked together.

When they reached Riley's car, Meredith just stood staring at her. Then he said, "You should have told me."

Riley was truly taken aback now. She didn't know how to reply.

Finally she said, "Would it have mattered?"

"That's not the point," Meredith said. "It wasn't your call. You should have told me. I've got to be in the loop."

They held each other's gazes for a moment.

Riley wondered …

Is this the only reprimand I'm going to get?

Then Riley said, "OK."

As she climbed into her car, Meredith added …

"You guys did a good job in Mississippi."

"Thanks," Riley said.

As she started to pull away, she saw that Meredith was still standing nearby watching her with folded arms. As she studied his expression, something started to dawn on her.

He cares about me.

He cares about Bill and Jenn too.

More than that, she sensed that Meredith admired the bond that had grown among Riley and her two partners—even when that bond meant covering for each other's foibles and mistakes.

Above all else, Riley sensed that Meredith was lonely—a lonely man in a lonely job.

He envies us, she thought. *He envies what we have.*

It seemed strange to her—strange and sad, but also somehow rather lovely.

She drove on past him and continued on her way home.

She thought that next time she would tell him about whatever she was doing.

*

Later that day, Riley and Blaine were sitting on her back deck watching their three girls playing with the dog and cat. They were sipping soft drinks and eating snacks that Gabriela had prepared to welcome Riley home.

Out of earshot of the kids, Riley had just finished explaining to Blaine what had happened with Jilly.

"Jesus," Blaine said. "She seems just fine now."

"I know," Riley said. "Let's hope it lasts. I think it will. She just needs a little help to get through things."

A silence fell between them.

Then Blaine said, "I knew something was wrong with Jilly when I drove your daughters home. But I ..."

His voice faded for a moment, and then he continued ...

"But I didn't know what to do or say. Should I have talked to her? Should I have tried to draw her out? I'm not her father—at least not yet. I don't know the boundaries. I don't know how to navigate all this. I don't know the rules."

"Neither do I," Riley said. "There's no instruction manual for what we're trying to do—putting our two families together."

They squeezed each other's hands and watched their children quietly for a few moments.

Then Blaine said, "I'd better get back to my restaurant."

Riley nodded and said, "I haven't slept in a long time. I may go to bed soon."

Riley and Blaine stood up and kissed each other lightly.

Blaine said, "Riley ... let's take things slowly. I mean, with you and me. Make sure we do it right."

"OK," Riley said, feeling a lump in her throat.

Blaine called for Crystal, and the two of them left. As Riley continued watching her two daughters playing, Blaine's words echoed through her head ...

"Let's take things slowly."

It sounded like such good advice. But no matter which way she looked, there were family emergencies to rush back for, murderous monsters to thwart and capture, dire matters of life and death, and crises that looked small but somehow seemed as desperately urgent as anything else in her life.

Riley sighed deeply and sadly and replayed those words again in her head ...

"Let's take things slowly."

She wished with all her heart that she could take all kinds of things slowly ...

If only life would let me.

ONCE SHUNNED
(A Riley Paige Mystery—Book 15)

"A masterpiece of thriller and mystery! The author did a magnificent job developing characters with a psychological side that is so well described that we feel inside their minds, follow their fears and cheer for their success. The plot is very intelligent and will keep you entertained throughout the book. Full of twists, this book will keep you awake until the turn of the last page."
--Books and Movie Reviews, Roberto Mattos (re Once Gone)

ONCE SHUNNED is book #15 in the bestselling Riley Paige mystery series, which begins with the #1 bestseller ONCE GONE (Book #1).

When a serial killer strikes across a series of towns and the only potential witness is unable to speak, it is up to FBI Special Agent Riley Paige to enter the mind of this complex man, and to learn what, if anything, he knows.

What do these victims have in common? What exactly did this man witness?

In this dark psychological suspense thriller, Riley Paige must battle her own demons as she is summoned to solve a crime that leaves all others stumped, one that will force her to enter, too deep, into the mind of a psychopath…..

An action-packed thriller with heart-pounding suspense, ONCE SHUNNED is book #15 in a riveting new series—with a beloved character—that will leave you turning pages late into the night.

Book #16 in the Riley Paige series will be available soon.

Blake Pierce

Blake Pierce is author of the bestselling RILEY PAGE mystery series, which includes fifteen books (and counting). Blake Pierce is also the author of the MACKENZIE WHITE mystery series, comprising nine books (and counting); of the AVERY BLACK mystery series, comprising six books; of the KERI LOCKE mystery series, comprising five books; of the MAKING OF RILEY PAIGE mystery series, comprising three books (and counting); of the KATE WISE mystery series, comprising two books (and counting); of the CHLOE FINE psychological suspense mystery, comprising three books (and counting); and of the JESSE HUNT psychological suspense thriller series, comprising three books (and counting).

An avid reader and lifelong fan of the mystery and thriller genres, Blake loves to hear from you, so please feel free to visit www.blakepierceauthor.com to learn more and stay in touch.

BEFORE HE SEES (Book #2)
BEFORE HE COVETS (Book #3)
BEFORE HE TAKES (Book #4)
BEFORE HE NEEDS (Book #5)
BEFORE HE FEELS (Book #6)
BEFORE HE SINS (Book #7)
BEFORE HE HUNTS (Book #8)
BEFORE HE PREYS (Book #9)
BEFORE HE LONGS (Book #10)

AVERY BLACK MYSTERY SERIES
CAUSE TO KILL (Book #1)
CAUSE TO RUN (Book #2)
CAUSE TO HIDE (Book #3)
CAUSE TO FEAR (Book #4)
CAUSE TO SAVE (Book #5)
CAUSE TO DREAD (Book #6)

KERI LOCKE MYSTERY SERIES
A TRACE OF DEATH (Book #1)
A TRACE OF MUDER (Book #2)
A TRACE OF VICE (Book #3)
A TRACE OF CRIME (Book #4)
A TRACE OF HOPE (Book #5)

CPSIA information can be obtained
at www.ICGtesting.com
Printed in the USA
LVHW051511110719
623803LV00016B/522